THE FLIGHT OF THE

EBONY OWL

THE FLIGHT OF THE
EBONY OWL

Jennifer Carswell Hynd

 ORCHARD BOOKS

ORCHARD BOOKS
96 Leonard Street, London EC2A 4RH
Orchard Books Australia
14 Mars Road, Lane Cove, NSW 2066
ISBN 1 86039 149 4 (hardback)
ISBN 1 86039 089 7 (paperback)
First published in hardback in Great Britain 1997
First published in paperback in Great Britain 1998
Text © Jennifer Carswell Hynd
1 2 3 4 5 6 02 01 00 99 98 97
The right of Jennifer Carswell Hynd to be identified
as the author of this work has been asserted by her in accordance with the
Copyright, Designs and Patents Act, 1988.
Printed in Great Britain

To my mum and dad
for all the years away

The Awakening

Something came flying through the darkness. A rush of air hit his face and he dropped to the floor of the cave a second before the skeleton of a huge bird, with a razor-sharp beak and web-like wings, swooped low over his prone body. He watched in horror, as suspended from the ceiling, the skeleton bird swung back into the darkness, even in death it seemed capable of attack.

Once his heart had stopped racing, he shone the flashlight up into the recesses of the dark cave which was decorated like an ancient burial chamber. The skeleton bird must have been hung there to guard the entrance from intruders. On the side walls hung many strange and eerie ceremonial masks, each one honed to the shape of a bird's skull, while at the back of the cave positioned upon a rock sat a rectangular box which seemed to be made of the same smooth metal as the masks. He eased open the lid of the box and a draught of musty air escaped. His fingers prized away the layers of dried leaves to reveal the statue of an owl

7

covered in grimy white feathers. Its black beak was small and curved, and the lids of its round eyes were tightly closed. He picked it up and, just like a child's doll, the owl's lids flickered and slowly opened. At that moment a tremor shook the ground beneath him, but the man felt nothing, so entranced was he by the owl's penetrating stare. Around him the masks clattered to the floor and the light from the owl's eyes intensified into pulsating orbs of emerald light. Trapped within the stream of light, he had no hope of escape. The owl's awakening had begun.

Only when the owl's eyes eventually dimmed did his senses return. The cave was now plunged into darkness, but in his mind that incredible green light burned furiously on. Cradling the box to his chest, he made for the mouth of the cave. Outside the familiar sound and smell of the sea filled his senses but then came another sound. He looked up, blinking rapidly in the light, to see a seagull flying at him, its white wings silhouetted black against the bright sun. The bird screeched at him in fury, and then he saw that a whole flock of birds were circling above him, as though they were angry at him for removing the owl from the cave.

He made for his car, only to find a black raven perched on its bonnet watching him keenly with its beady yellow eyes. He shooed at it and the bird flew up until, hovering high above the car, it opened its beak to screech loudly and dropped a large stone. The stone hurtled downwards cracking the windscreen on impact. The car alarm went off with a shrill scream.

At that same moment a dark-haired boy on his paper round cycled around the corner in time to see the bird drop the stone. He was so intent on watching that he did not see the man open his car door and the bike collided with it, the handlebars gouging a deep scratch in the paintwork. He saw a metal box drop from the man's hands as he fell in a cascade of newspapers. Then the man was looming over him with a strange demented look in his eyes. "You'll pay for this," he hissed angrily as the boy tried to back away. The man bent quickly to retrieve the box and, in that second, the boy picked up his bike and pedalled away along the seafront as fast as he could.

With the encased owl safely under his arm, the man stared at the badly dented door. "I'll have the police on to you," he shouted after the boy. Growling under his breath, he got into his car and drove away, unaware that the large black raven followed him all the way back to his house on the cliffs.

1
The Sighting

"Och, there's a horrible great beastie up on the cliffs," old Angus McDermott was shouting. "It was like a ghostly warrior from another world," he said, his eyes growing wide with fear.

"Away, with yer havers, Angus," a man in the crowd shouted back, but Angus just waggled his bony finger at him.

"It stood nine foot tall and carried a lance that looked as sharp as a butcher's cleaver." He halted for a moment to regain his breath and dab at his face. "And it wore a strange mask on its face. Och, you should have seen it! And there was a huge black crow that sat on its shoulder with..."

Angus didn't get a chance to finish because the crowd had begun to laugh at him.

Meanwhile eleven-year-old Jamie Logan was making

the most of the last week of his summer holidays. He had been fishing from the other side of the pier when he heard Angus's voice. Normally, with his crinkly smile and salty humour, old Angus McDermott told of his adventures at sea but that morning his voice was shaky and troubled. Jamie put down his fishing rod and wandered over to join the villagers who had gathered around Angus on the pier. Pushing through to the front of the crowd he saw the old man shake his head furiously and mop his brow with an old hanky. Although he was puffing furiously on his pipe, Jamie could now see that he had forgotten to light it.

"Angus, this is no' the time for April Fool's tricks," a man said, "you're just having us on."

But Jamie, intrigued by Angus's words, wanted to hear more. "Go on Angus, tell us what happened," he shouted, trying to be heard over the rest of the crowd.

"I didnae wait around to find out. I turned and ran until I thought my lungs were going to burst." Angus stopped to dab at his watery eyes again. "I havenae run that fast in forty year."

Several American tourists who had joined the group were chuckling among themselves but Jamie knew that although Angus sometimes stretched the truth, he had never come up with a story like this before. But it was the look on Angus's face that really worried him. He didn't think Angus was making it up at all. But then his thoughts were broken as the midday ferry tooted loudly on its approach to the harbour. Around him, the crowd began to disperse.

"C'mon you guys," one of the Americans said as the ferry docked. "Let's go find someone who's got real Scottish stories to tell."

"He's probably had one too many of those drams of whisky they drink up here," another man wearing a baseball cap said laughing. "He'll be telling us he's seen the Loch Ness monster next."

As the crowd drifted away, Angus walked over and slumped down on to the seat where Jamie had been fishing peacefully only a minute before.

"Is all this true, Angus?" Jamie asked him and the old man nodded his head in reply.

"I wouldnae lie about something like this, Jamie," he said. "I've got a bad feeling about..."

Suddenly a seagull screeched loudly and flew at Angus's head. The old man shivered and stood up, pulling his coat closer to his body even though it was a warm late summer morning. He grabbed Jamie by the arm. "It is as though something has been woken up that 'til now has lain peaceful," he stated firmly.

Just as Jamie was about to ask what he meant, he was forced to shut his eyes tightly as a sudden gust of cold wind blew stronger. Soon it had turned into a small swirling tornado that tossed dirt and litter around both their heads. Angus gave a loud screech and backed away, leaving Jamie shielding his eyes from the dust. "I want no more to do with this," Angus shouted as he stumbled away from Jamie along the seafront with the wind whipping along behind him.

"Angus! Be careful!" Jamie yelled, as he watched the old man glance around nervously, the cold wind catching at his coat tails. Flung about like a puppet on a string, Angus's arms and legs went in all directions as he tried to regain his balance. Finally, in an effort to escape, Angus ran into a bus shelter and covered his head with his hands. Jamie watched in disbelief as the wind whirled up rubbish around him, for a moment obscuring him completely from view. Then, just as suddenly, the wind died away as though it had grown bored with the chase.

Jamie, his heart still hammering in his chest, did not see the waves in the harbour grow choppy as another blustery gale blew in from nowhere. Across the top of the waves it came, causing the anchored boats to strain and toss against their moorings like the heads of tethered horses. Then it reached the quay, rippling across the wooden boards and flinging the hovering seagulls up into the air in a chaos of wings. All Jamie could do was stand among the flurry of flapping wings and sharp cries as the wind billowed around him.

It was only when a gull's sharp feathered wing struck his forehead that Jamie began to feel afraid. He shouted and threw up his arm and at that moment he felt that he was being watched closely. He swung around and his eyes focused on the faint outline of a face in the midst of the swirling cloud. He backed away in fright as two pale yellow eyes with the largest and darkest pupils Jamie had ever seen probed his face deeply. Then the gusting wind died away and the face disappeared. The birds settled back down on the pier squabbling angrily over the fishing bait as if nothing had happened. Jamie listened to their harsh calls, feeling that the wind had ruffled more than just their feathers.

He glanced up at the locals going about their business along the harbour, but they did not seem to have noticed anything unusual. In the distance he could see Angus heading for home, and Jamie felt an uneasiness settle over him. Maybe Angus was right, maybe something had been awakened.

Gathering up his fishing gear hurriedly, Jamie cycled away from the pier, leaving the remainder of the maggots for the quarrelling gulls.

2

Murphy

Craiginver was a small fishing village on the west coast of Scotland where Jamie had lived all his life. His mum ran a café on the seafront and his older sister did all she could to annoy him. Their dad had died when Jamie was very young, in the days when Craiginver had been a quiet place. But things had changed since then; now the village was filled with the faces of strangers, as more and more tourists flocked there every summer. Hotels had sprung up and restaurants had opened. Out in the harbour in a less hurried world, a dwindling number of fishing boats, just like the one Jamie's dad had once worked on, still came and went just as they had before tourism invaded the tiny village.

But that summer the fishing boats were in danger of disappearing completely. A London businessman called Murphy had arrived in town with big plans to build a lavish new marina. He didn't want local fishing boats mooring there – just pleasure craft filled with rich people who would spend their money in his new hotel and restaurants. No one had thought when he bought the land under the cliffs at the very north end of the harbour that such a plan could be possible. But Murphy had lots of money to spend and a lot of promises for the locals. "There'll be plenty of jobs and money in everyone's pockets," he told the villagers when his plans were made public. Some tried to voice their doubts but Murphy wasn't going to be stopped easily. He soon had bulldozer teams hard at work changing the shape of Craiginver's little harbour forever.

Around the same time he purchased old Mrs McGregor's white house up on the cliff top into which he moved, along with two security guards and their large black dogs. For several weeks rumours spread about how he'd made his money. It was even said that he'd paid cash for the house, but nobody really knew the truth, which made the stories grow wilder by the day. The latest rumour to spread through the village was that all work had come to a halt at the marina after part of the cliff had fallen away revealing a deep cave. Murphy had instructed his workers to build a tall wire fence to keep people out. No one, not even his workers, were allowed near until further notice.

So far, Jamie had had little to do with the mysterious Murphy, until that is, his best friend, the fearless Fergus Montgomerie had crashed his bike into Murphy's black

Range Rover. Fergo had told Jamie about the incident, making him vow not to tell anyone. "I've never seen anyone act like that before," Fergo had said. "He'll be after me to pay for it, I know he will." Fergo had gulped nervously and shivered. Jamie had never seen his normally unflappable friend like that before. He was now so scared of being recognised by Murphy that he had refused to go fishing with Jamie on the pier in case he was spotted. Instead he was going to lay low until things calmed down.

But Jamie was keen to tell Fergo what had happened to Angus so he went to find him. He pedalled as fast as he could away from the pier. He cycled past Murphy's new marina and around the bay, to the last undisturbed cove in Craiginver; one of the few places Murphy had not managed to get his hands on.

There were no expensive yachts moored here, only old fishing boats that through time had come to resemble the driftwood that floated ashore around them. Jamie knew the cove was Fergo's favourite place. He propped his bike against the two upturned dinghies at the cove's rocky entrance and ran over the shingle towards an old dilapidated boat shed at the other end. Fergo was nowhere to be seen, but as Jamie got nearer, he spotted Fergo's shabby old coat draped over the hull of a battered dinghy and heard the faint scraping sound of sandpaper.

"Fergo!" he yelled at the top of his voice.

A head of dark curly hair appeared behind the roughened hull of the old dinghy and the sanding noise stopped abruptly. Two dark eyes, then the whole round impish face of Fergo appeared. He glanced up warily at Jamie's approach and scanned the beach to see if anyone had followed him. He scowled at Jamie, his eyebrows knitting together under his unruly fringe. He was not pleased to be found.

"What are you doing here?" he asked gruffly.

Jamie ignored the tone of his friend's voice. "You won't believe what's happened..." Jamie began, but he didn't get a chance to finish.

"Has Murphy decided to leave town?" Fergo asked. For a moment his eyes lit up but Jamie shook his head.

"No," he replied, "it's something very strange." Jamie opened his mouth to continue but he could tell from the frown on Fergo's face that his friend wasn't in the mood to believe in a pair of ghostly eyes in a windstorm. Jamie decided to just tell him about Angus and the warrior on the cliffs – at least there were others who had heard this story as well.

Fergo was getting impatient. "So, what's your news then?"

"Angus saw a ghostly beastie up on the cliff path last night." Jamie said it so seriously that Fergo couldn't help but scoff.

"And now I suppose you're going to tell me your mum's won the lottery! I thought you were being serious." He turned his back and went back to sanding the dinghy and for a moment Jamie didn't know what to do next. He had been sure that Fergo would be interested, as nothing usually happened in the village. He decided to tell him just a little more.

"Angus said he saw a masked warrior carrying a lance as sharp as a butcher's cleaver – " But even this didn't bring a flicker of interest to Fergo's face – "and I don't think he made it up because I've never seen Angus look so scared before."

All Fergo did was scrape the sandpaper faster, and so as a last resort, Jamie told him the whole story. He told him about the birds attacking him on the pier and about the peculiar face in the mist. "It was as though it was looking for me. I'm going up to the cliffs myself tomorrow…and I thought you might come with me?" he added finally.

Fergo instantly stopped sanding and stared up at his friend. "You'll no catch me up there, ghosts or no ghosts," he stated firmly. "Murphy lives up there now and I bet he could chew up Angus's stupid ghost and swallow it for breakfast."

Jamie sighed loudly. He had hoped that Fergo would have shown just a little enthusiasm by the time he had finished the story. Normally he would have jumped at the chance for a bit of adventure, but everything had changed since his stupid accident with Murphy.

Jamie dug the toe of his shoe into the sand. He didn't think ghost hunting was going be much fun on his own. "Maybe the others are right…maybe you *are* a fearty. Just a big fearty!" he teased.

"No, I'm no'!" Fergo retorted hotly. "But you won't catch me anywhere near Murphy again."

"He doesn't even know who you are," Jamie laughed. "Maybe you could hide here until you're old enough to grow a beard. He wouldn't recognise you then."

Fergo bristled and his face began to turn red. He clambered up to stand on top of the upturned dinghy. "I'm not scared of him but I know that if he catches me, he'll make me pay for the damage to his car. Anyway, he gives me the creeps!" he declared defiantly.

"Well, prove you're not scared and come up to the cliffs with me," Jamie replied.

But Fergo, still frowning, shook his head. He couldn't understand why Jamie was getting so riled over one of Angus's old stories; especially one about a stupid ghost.

"I've got better things to do than go after a giant ghost with a butcher's cleaver."

"As *sharp* as a butcher's cleaver was all Angus said," Jamie retorted.

"Makes no difference. I like my body the way it is – in one piece!"

Fergo's eyebrows knitted into a straight line and Jamie knew that he was not going to change his mind, no matter how hard he tried to convince him.

"He's put fear into your veins instead of blood," Jamie goaded. But Fergo didn't even bother to reply, his scowl said everything. He turned his back on Jamie and went back to sanding the hull of the old boat. For several seconds neither of them spoke but it was Jamie who finally turned away.

"I'll be at home if you change your mind," he said.

And he stalked off up the beach trying hard to convince himself that he would be better off on his own. In this mood, Jamie thought, Fergo would just get in the way.

3
The Dream

That night Jamie had the dream again. But only once before could he remember it being so vivid and real – and that had been shortly after his dad had died. At first, he could only remember fragments of the dream but as it continued, it slowly came back to him. In the past, if he got up and found his dad's lucky charm, the dream would go away but tonight the star-shaped pendant seemed powerless to help him. As soon as his eyes closed he was deep within the dream again and this time, Jamie could not break himself free.

Alone, in the middle of an open moor he stood listening as a faint beat of a drum could be heard in the wind. He turned his head towards the sound and slowly his eyes focused on the skyline where a line of tall warriors were advancing towards him through the heather, some holding banners, others shields and spears. Jamie knew a battle was about to begin as these tall warriors began to march faster towards him, their banners stretching out against the sky. Only then did he see that painted on these banners was a great black owl, with the greenest eyes he could ever imagine. To him, that was more scary than the shouts of the approaching army. Then as he watched a dark cloud appeared behind them which, as it grew closer, Jamie realised was not a cloud at all, but a flock of large fierce birds flying in formation.

At this point, Jamie usually fought to wake from the dream before the birds or the warriors reached him, but tonight he couldn't. The images were so strong, so real, there was little he could do. The warriors were almost upon him, their warlike cries and the thud of their great feet echoing louder and louder in his head when suddenly the battlefield faded and all Jamie was left with was the image of an owl in front of him. Then a second later its eyes were replaced by the two pale yellow eyes which he had seen that day on the pier.

Jamie tried with all his heart to think of something different and make the face go away, but the haunted eyes with the blackest pupils just continued to stare straight into his own. Jamie tossed in his sleep and cried out loudly.

Meanwhile, out in the garden, a yellow-eyed raven had landed on the garden gate and was watching Jamie's window. It flew up to land on the window ledge and then it began to peck at the glass.

Jamie heard the tapping and woke. He sat up abruptly to see the raven sitting on his windowsill. He forgot the dream as he got up to shoo the bird away. It flew off to perch in the apple tree in the garden. Jamie, his mind still fuddled with sleep, watched the bird settle in the tree but then he heard a voice echoing throughout his room. He whirled around to see where it was coming from but there was no one there. Hiding behind the curtains, he peered out into the garden and this time he saw a tall shrouded figure beckoning to him. Its lips were forming words, and Jamie could hear what it was saying to him through the closed window.

"Find the Ebony Owl. The time has come," it told him firmly.

"Who are you? What do you want?" Jamie yelled. Then he rubbed his eyes and peered out nervously again, only to find the ghostly face and the mist had disappeared completely. He let his breath out with relief, but a second later the black raven had fluttered back to the windowsill to stare at him with its bright yellow eyes. He tried to scare it away, but this time it refused to budge and instead, in a flurry of wings, it tapped its shiny black beak against the window pecking a hole through the glass. A small shard flew straight towards Jamie who only had time to put his hand up to his face to shield himself.

He had forgotten that he was still holding his dad's cherished pendant. Its four metal points were between his fingers, the centre facing outwards in the palm of his hand. That was what stopped the shard from piercing his hand. Instead of feeling pain, all Jamie felt was the four points bend inwards as the glass shard stabbed into the metal. Then Jamie felt heat in his palm. He threw the pendant as hard as he could at the window. It hit, cracking the glass and causing the raven, still sitting on the ledge outside, to shriek in alarm. Jamie watched it fly off, and it looked as if the tips of its wings were smoking.

Meanwhile the pendant had bounced down on to the carpet and under his chest of drawers. Jamie bent down to pick it up but he could see that now it had a round hole in the centre where the glass shard had pierced it. Jamie stretched out his hand and without touching it, the pendant flew into his hand. The pendant was icy and it stuck to the palm of his hand, burning him and leaving an imprint. He dropped it as quickly as he could and went back to his bed and just lay there; the sting from the ice-cold burn causing his eyes to water. Blinking away the tears, he shook his hand and glanced up at the window only to see that his window pane was now intact.

Jamie shivered and scrambled across the room to place his good hand on the smooth unbroken window pane. There was no sign of any crack or hole and when he looked out into the garden there was no sign that anything had been there. Was it a dream or had some sort of magic just taken place? He glanced down at the pendant which lay face up on the carpet, but was too scared to pick it up again. Jamie lay awake for many hours that night. He was too frightened to go back to sleep in case anything else happened.

When he awoke the next morning it took a second before he remembered all that had happened. He recalled seeing the face of the ghostly apparition and then he remembered the raven in the garden and what had happened to his dad's pendant. From his bed he cautiously glanced towards the window but the pane of glass was not broken. He got out of bed and ventured over to the window, where the pendant was lying on the carpet. Gingerly, he picked it up. It was no longer cold, but the small round hole was still there. Jamie glanced nervously out of the window only to see sparrows and black birds scrounging for worms in the dewy grass. He stared down at the palm of his hand and gently touched his palm, rubbing away a circle of dried blood to see the small star-shaped scar. So it really had been more than a dream.

He stayed in his room all morning. His whole hand ached and his heart raced every time he thought of what had happened the night before. Eventually, his mum came up to find out what was wrong.

"Are you ill?" she asked, touching his brow.

"No," Jamie replied, hiding his wounded hand under the covers. He could not bring himself to tell her what had happened. She looked closely at his face and decided that he was a little pale.

"If your no' feeling well, you'd better come down to the café so that I can keep an eye on you," she said as she peered at his tongue and pulled down his lower eyelids. "But I think it's just a breath of fresh air you need."

Jamie shook his head. He did not want any fresh air until he was sure there would be no savage yellow-eyed ravens ready to attack him. He closed his hand and felt the pain seer through it, and realised that somehow he had to make Fergo believe the story.

"Och, no. What happened here?" he heard his mum ask. Only then did he realise that the pendant was now lying beside him on the blanket. Before he could reach it, his mum had picked it up and was peering at it closely.

"Jamie, what have you done to this?" she asked seeing the wee hole in its centre. "This is hardly the way to treat your dad's precious pendant. It's an ancient family heirloom, given to him by your granddad, and his before that," she scolded him. "Heaven knows how long its been in the family."

"I know that, and it wasn't my fault," Jamie said angrily.

"Well, if you can't take care of it I'll take it away until you're old enough to look after it properly," she said, but Jamie snatched it back.

"You can't, Dad gave it to *me*, it's mine now."

Jamie jumped from his bed, anxious that his mum should leave.

"Jamie, sometimes I don't know what to do with you," his mum said irritably. "Come and make yourself useful down at the café."

"Och, Mum, I've got to talk to Fergo. It's really important I see him," he told her.

"Then there cannae be *that* much wrong with you," she replied.

As soon as his mum left, Jamie got dressed and putting the pendant safely in his pocket, he set off for the cove. It was time Fergo knew everything. But he couldn't help but wonder how he was going to make Fergo believe him.

Once at the cove, he walked down the deserted beach calling out Fergo's name and although no one answered, he thought he could feel someone's eyes on him. He stopped suddenly, turning to look up the beach for his friend, completely unaware of the spiralling wind coming in towards him over the waves. He didn't see the misty cloud with the shrouded figure in its midst stepping out of the swell and wading on to the shore.

By the time Jamie reached the boat sheds the windswept shape had followed him up the sandy beach and, although it was barely visible, its great heavy feet caused enormous craters to appear in the sand. At that moment Jamie shouted out Fergo's name as he finally spied him going into the very last boat shed.

Jamie ran up towards Fergo and the footprints followed him up past the old wrecked boats towards the rocks that sat behind the sheds. The figure beckoned to Jamie silently but he did not turn and so it began to call to him. Before Jamie reached Fergo, he finally heard the calls and he turned back to face the sea.

"What's wrong?" Fergo asked him but Jamie did not reply. He was scanning the horizon to see who was calling his name but then an intense beam of light projected out from the face in the mist and probed Jamie's face. All Fergo felt was an icy draught. Jamie could hear

Fergo shouting in the background but he seemed a long way away. All that mattered was watching the light.

For several seconds Jamie was held in the ghostly beam before the shrouded figure began to speak to him. The words vibrated out in a chilly breeze that intensified around Jamie's head.

"Jamie. You are the one," the voice began. "Only you can help us." Now Jamie could see its eyes clearly. "Go to the cliffs. You must rescue the Ebony Owl."

"Who are you?" Jamie yelled at the top of his voice.

"At the cliffs, Jamie, the answer lies there," came the voice again.

"Leave me alone!" Jamie screamed out.

By this stage Fergo thought his friend had gone completely crazy. He went to shake Jamie but just as he made a grab at him, his mouth filled with sand which had been whipped up by a sudden gust of wind.

Blinded by the swirling sand, Fergo heard Jamie give a faint cry. He could see him standing in the midst of a whirling, twirling, sand-filled tornado. Then Jamie fell to the ground, coughing and spluttering and Fergo ran forward, breaking the ghostly figure's beam of light. Jamie felt the chill wind stop and when he glanced upwards, all he saw was Fergo's outline and his worried face peering down at him through a curtain of grainy sand.

Jamie staggered to his feet, his eyes smarting from the coating of sand that covered him from head to toe. He shook his head and slowly his vision cleared. Fergo was still staring at him with his back towards the sea. Jamie's eyes focused just in time to see the giant footsteps retreating back towards the waves. The marks lasted for only a second as a wave came in over the yellow sand, washing them away. Jamie tried to speak but instead he coughed up sand and grit. He pointed the marks out to Fergo, who ran forward but was too late as the foamy white wave smoothed out the sand. Fergo glanced back at Jamie who was still spitting out sand.

"What's going on?" he asked worriedly.

"My dream, it's becoming real! And there's a voice — you've got to believe me Fergo — it told me to find an Ebony Owl!" Jamie cried out.

Fergo looked at him unbelievingly. "And what's an Ebony Owl?" he asked incredulously.

"That's just it. I don't know," Jamie replied, but then he bent down to search the sand. "But did you see those giant footsteps? They were right here!"

Jamie pointed down at the now smooth, sandy beach.

Fergo shrugged. "I saw something but it was hard to tell what it was. Everything happened so quickly."

At that moment a seagull flew up from the rocks. Both boys jumped when they heard the flurry of wings as the bird swooped over their heads with inches to spare. Jamie dived on to the sand, covering his head with his hands expecting it to attack them.

Fergo looked at him anxiously and then at the seagull which was now flying away over the sea.

"Jamie, what is going on?" Fergo whispered when Jamie finally got up.

"You'll have to trust me," Jamie explained. "I need to find out what the Ebony Owl is."

"Och, you're having me on!" Fergo said. "Anyway, voices and dreams can't hurt you."

"Yes they can," Jamie declared. Catching his breath he explained how the raven's beak had shattered his bedroom window and how his dad's pendant had saved him. He turned his palm over to expose the small wound. Fergo gazed at it for a few moments before he spoke.

"Jamie, I saw a big black bird like that down at the harbour, the same morning I had the run-in with Murphy."

Jamie looked straight at his friend. "So, you do believe me?" he asked, but his friend wouldn't admit it. He was unwilling to get involved in anything that might take him close to Murphy again.

"What did your mum say about the broken window?" Fergo asked changing the subject.

"When I woke up, there wasn't even a scratch on it," Jamie said with a sigh.

"There you are then. It was just a dream!"

"No, it wasn't Fergo!" he replied firmly. "You have to believe me."

Fergo didn't reply. He could tell that this was no joke to Jamie. He really seemed scared. "Well, maybe we should get out of here before any more of your dreams come true," he said grabbing Jamie by the coat and hauling him up the beach and away from the cove.

4
The Search

Once back in the safety of his kitchen, Jamie tried to describe to Fergo what he had seen on the beach, but when he glanced over, Fergo seemed more interested in the contents of their biscuit tin.

"So you think this owl might be up on the cliffs then?" Fergo asked, with nearly a whole piece of Jamie's mum's homemade shortbread in his mouth.

"The voice told me that that was where I would find it," Jamie replied. "And remember, yesterday Angus saw something strange up there." He looked at Fergo searchingly. "I've got to go and have a look. Will you come too?"

Fergo hesitated and screwed up his face. "It's a bit of a hike up there."

"Fergo, this is serious," Jamie replied. There was a look of fear in his eyes and Fergo realised that his friend really believed a strange ghostly warrior had spoken to him.

"Okay, I'll come, but only to prove to you that there aren't such things as ghosts, especially ones that ask you to find ebony owls," he said, his eyebrows lowering into a thoughtful line. "Taking photographs might be a way to prove what it really is. How about asking Fiona for her camera?"

But Jamie didn't think asking his sister for her precious camera was such a good idea. "We'd have to tell her why we wanted it and then she'd want to come with us...she'd never let me take her camera out on my own."

"We could always sacrifice her to your ghostly warrior if things turned nasty!"

For a brief moment Jamie thought this idea had possibilities. It was one way of getting rid of his interfering sister but then he saw the flaw in the plan.

"Even if she was being bitten to death by blood-sucking vampires," said Jamie, shaking his head, "she still wouldn't let me get my hands on that camera."

"What else can we do then?" said Fergo.

Jamie stared out of the kitchen window while Fergo sat down to think with another piece of shortbread.

"Maybe the Ghostbusters could sell us an ectoplasm trap instead," Fergo said through a mouthful of biscuit.

"Be serious, Fergo. That was just an old film, and those weren't even real ghosts."

At that moment they were distracted from their problems when the back door opened and a tall girl with a mass of long curly red hair walked in. Her eyes were the same bright blue as Jamie's.

33

"Isn't it a scream?" she laughed. "Angus has seen a ghostly warrior on the cliffs! Everyone at the *Herald* is talking about it and even the police are going up to investigate." Picking up a biscuit she flopped down into a kitchen chair beside Fergo. "It's hardly going to be a ghost up there though is it? More like an old tramp that Angus has mistaken in the gloom."

Fourteen-year-old Fiona wanted to be a newspaper reporter when she left school and that summer she had managed to get some work experience at the *Craiginver Herald*. Although she just did odd jobs, she kept hoping that someone might notice her talent and assign her to write a story; but so far no one had.

Meanwhile Jamie was giving Fergo a knowing look which meant "don't say a word", but Fergo was pretending not to notice. He liked Fiona, who always seemed so strong and courageous.

"What are you two doing anyway?" Fiona asked catching her brother's furtive glance, but before Jamie had a chance to speak Fergo blurted it all out. "Jamie and I are doing our own investigation into the warrior," he declared importantly.

Jamie groaned when Fiona burst out laughing. Why did Fergo always have to open his mouth at the wrong time? He knew it only helped Fiona make fun of them. And why did Fergo even like Fiona? She was three years older, and nearly a foot taller than him, but this didn't seem to deter Fergo in the slightest. He was always trying to impress her.

Jamie tried to muffle Fergo but before he could stop him, the words were out of Fergo's mouth. "We need to borrow a camera...Maybe we could take yours? We promise to be careful with it!" he stated bluntly.

Jamie, bright red in the face, looked at his sister but luckily she hadn't taken the idea seriously. "My camera's too good to be used on one of your wild-goose chases...or should I say 'ghost' chases." She carried on laughing while Jamie kicked Fergo hard under the table.

"Ouch," he cried, rubbing his leg and glaring at Jamie.

Fiona didn't take any notice but just sat there crunching on her biscuit. "I really can't believe you've been taken in by all this. Old Angus's stories get more and more far-fetched every week, and here you are believing his biggest fairy tale yet." As Fiona shook her head, Jamie felt a small ball of anger begin to grow inside him.

"I don't think Angus made it up at all," he said defiantly, hoping his face wouldn't turn red again.

"But you can't honestly believe it's a ghost he's seen? And, anyway, who would be mean enough to scare old Angus?" Fiona asked.

"The only person I can think of is that horrible man, Murphy," Fergo declared. "It could be him in a costume for all we know, keeping people away from that house of his."

At that moment Fiona stopped chewing and a thoughtful look came over her face.

"Fergo, that could be the first sound idea that's ever entered your head!" she said.

But Jamie wanted to tell her that she was wrong. He glanced at his sister and could tell by the way she was biting her nails that her mind was now working frantically.

When she looked up at Jamie, her eyes were bright with excitement. "Fergo could be right. This could be Murphy's doing," she stated firmly. "C'mon, get your coats, I'm coming up to the cliffs with you. This could lead to my first story, my big break!"

Jamie didn't move. "Fiona what are you talking about?" he asked.

"Don't you see? Murphy might be employing somebody to scare people away from that house of his on the cliffs. People say that there's been a lot of late night activity up at that house since he arrived. Fergo could be right. He could be hiding something up there that he doesn't want anyone to see."

Jamie could feel his face turning red again with anger. "What about the voice, Fiona? How did Murphy conjure that up?" Now it was his turn to look searchingly from his sister to Fergo. "I think you are both wrong. This has nothing to do with Murphy!"

For a second Fiona looked at him as though his brain had turned to mush. "What voice?" she asked him.

"It's a long story," he replied quietly, and then reluctantly he told her about his dreams, of the face of the black owl that rippled on the banner and how strange magical incidents had started to happen since he had spoken with Angus on the quay. He even told her about what had happened to their dad's pendant but she wouldn't listen. She scoffed loudly.

"I remember Dad telling us those stories about magic and sorcery when you were really little. He told us that we came from a long line of sorcerers but they were just stories, Jamie, stories for bedtime." Then she turned to Fergo. "What do you think Fergo? Do you think there really is an 'Ebony Owl' up there that Jamie's meant to find?"

Fergo had been trying to keep out of the argument but both Jamie and Fiona were staring at him waiting for an answer. He didn't want to take sides. "I don't know. It could be Murphy up to no good, but Jamie seems pretty convinced..." Fergo's voice petered out under Fiona's look of contempt.

"Och, you're both hopeless," she replied. "You can look for your stupid owl if you want to," she said turning to Jamie, "but I'm looking for the logical explanation." She then stormed out of the room to get her camera leaving Jamie protesting loudly.

Fergo leaned over towards him. "Look on the bright side, now we get the camera and a photographer," he whispered.

5
The Path to the Cliffs

It was getting towards dusk when the three of them finally made it to the start of the cliff path. They each carried a small rucksack containing extra jumpers in case it got cold, while Fergo stuffed a few Mars bars into his coat pocket for good measure.

As Jamie gazed up at the cliff above them he felt as though they were setting off into uncharted territory rather than just venturing up the old familiar path that had been used for as long as anyone could remember. His mouth had turned dry and he felt for the pendant in his pocket. What if the warrior really was waiting for him? What did it want him to do? He played with the points between his fingers and tried to feel reassured, but ever since the raven attack, he knew that things were different. Having his dad's pendant made him feel safer, but it didn't stop him feeling a little bit scared.

"Have you changed your mind?" Fergo asked, nudging him, and the boys stared at each other. Then Jamie glanced at Fiona who didn't look scared at all.

"No," Jamie replied flatly, and with the evening sun setting the ocean ablaze with streaks of yellow and orange light, he set off first.

When they reached the top of the path which led them through a grove of silver birch trees, Jamie scanned the ground searching for signs of the giant footprints he had seen in the sand at the cove. Fergo kept a lookout through the trees on the right, beyond which lay the glen and the drove road that led on to the moor. Meanwhile, Fiona watched a family out with their dog for an evening stroll. The family walked past them laughing and joking and they certainly did not look as though they had seen a terrifying beastie from another ghostly world.

As they continued to walk on through the silent trees, Jamie began to hope that it was all a dream after all, or just one of Angus's stories. But soon the thin pale tree trunks of the birches were replaced by a tall thick hedge bounded by a strand of spiky barbed wire across the top. Though this path was used by the public, everything beyond the hedge was Murphy's private property.

"This is the start of Murphy's land," Fiona announced as they trudged on.

Fergo slowed down. He knew this only too well. A look of dismay appeared on his face when he noticed the menacing black dog with snarling white teeth on the trespass signs that hung on the hedge. He ran after the other two shouting, "Maybe this isn't such a good idea?"

Fiona did not hear him, she was trying to make a hole in the hedge large enough to see through. She was muttering away as she tried to wriggle through the hedge backwards.

Jamie glanced up at Fergo, he could tell he was beginning to get very uneasy that he might bump into Murphy.

"I don't think we'll find a boy scout with a budgie up here," mumbled Fergo, "let alone a giant ghostly beastie with a black crow. I think we should forget the whole thi..."

But his plea was interrupted by Jamie who had dropped to his knees to investigate a small pile of feathers.

"Do ghostly birds drop feathers?" asked Jamie looking at the dark and shiny pile.

Fiona disentangled herself from her attempts to clamber through the hedge and came over to look. "Probably just an unlucky bird caught by a stoat or a cat," she said looking over his shoulder.

Meanwhile, Fergo had stumbled on a few paces. "Come and look at this," he said pointing shakily at a deep imprint in the ground. "It's a giant footprint!"

Jamie darted over and stared down to where Fergo was pointing. "It's like the ones on the sand," he whispered quietly. Jamie placed his foot inside the print. The soil was damp and his foot sank down into a print that was four times the size of his own. But unlike the shape of a human foot with five toes, there were only four indentations where its huge claw like talons had dug into the earth.

Uneasily, the three of them began to follow the tracks which were now easy to see in the damp ground. Suddenly there was the eerie screech of a bird high in the birch trees above them.

"What was that?" Fiona asked, grabbing Jamie's arm.

It was not the sound of a thrush or a curlew, but more like the harsh cry of a bird of prey.

"I don't know. It sounded like a hawk."

"Whatever it was, it sounded hungry!"

"Shh, quiet," Jamie whispered as a movement on the path ahead caught his eye. All three of them ducked behind the trunk of an old pine tree.

"Who's going to look?" Fiona whispered.

Fergo being the least hidden by the tree, didn't have much choice. He swallowed hard and taking a small step, he poked his head out. Then he darted back, nearly knocking Jamie and Fiona over in the process.

"There's something out there. It's really big...like a huge great beastie!"

Fiona grabbed Jamie so hard he began to lose the feeling in the fingers of his right arm and as she wasn't about to let go, they were forced to edge out together to see if Fergo was right.

"Let go of me and take a photo," Jamie whispered to Fiona who, still locked on to his sleeve, was not moving at all. All she could do was stare at the tall masked figure that stood scanning the horizon on the very edge of the cliff. It looked more ancient and ghostly than anything even old Angus could have described. Luckily, it did not glance in their direction, but stood staring out to sea resting its leg on a fallen pine tree at the very edge of the cliff. It held a long metal lance tightly in one hand and, as the three of them continued to stare silently at it, they could see that its body was completely draped in a long feathery cloak from shoulder to ankle. They could just see its massive trunk-like legs beneath the cloak. They seemed to be covered with woven leaves and over that was strapped roughly-hewn leather thongs all the way to its thighs. On its face was a metal mask in the shape of a bird's skull that obscured its features completely.

Jamie jumped as the yellow-eyed raven flew down to land on its left shoulder. It made the eerie sound they had heard earlier and echoed up through the trees and into the evening sky. Both warrior and bird seemed oblivious to their presence as they scanned the horizon.

Jamie and Fiona were still staring with open mouths when Fergo came up and tapped Fiona on the shoulder.

"Have you taken a photo yet?" he hissed. Fiona nearly jumped a foot in the air, but the fright brought her to her senses, and she hurriedly found the camera in her bag.

"Don't use the flash," Jamie remarked.

"I know, I know!" she said focusing the lens. At that moment the raven gave its evil call and then flapping its great black wings, it rose into the air and headed straight towards them. Fergo panicked and as he lost his balance he toppled backwards, grabbing the hood of Fiona's sweatshirt as he tried to save himself. The camera shutter went off with a loud click in the still evening as they both tumbled to the ground. Jamie grabbed Fergo's mouth to stop him shouting, while Fiona, twisting to save her camera from the fall, found herself trapped within the folds of Fergo's musty old coat.

The bird, landing in a birch tree not far above them, tilted its narrow black head and blinked its beady yellow eyes as it looked for the source of the noise. Even though they were partially hidden and lying absolutely still, its keen eyes soon pinpointed them. It spread its black wings and swooped down.

Jamie held his breath, terrified that the bird was going to alert the warrior to their presence. He glanced up thankfully to see the warrior continuing its vigil out over the cliffs and not taking any notice of its winged companion. For several moments Jamie watched the warrior as it pulled back its feather cloak to reveal a rough leather jerkin beneath. He also noticed that strapped to its leaf-clad legs was a leather water bottle and a small dagger held in a scabbard at its waist. He watched as it placed its hands on its hips and began to fill its lungs with air, its chest and shoulders expanding outwards as it inhaled. After nearly a minute the warrior slowly exhaled, causing a breeze to shake the leaves in the trees. A dim green light began to filter out from behind its mask and slowly became brighter and brighter, until it was reaching far out to sea like the beam of light from a cliff-top lighthouse.

"What's it doing?" Fergo asked in his quietest whisper.

"It's like its giving out a signal," Fiona suggested as she

43

looked out towards the isles.

Meanwhile, as the raven continued to swoop around them, the warrior stopped its vigil and rose up to its full height turning in their direction.

"We've had it now," Fergo squeaked, trying to make himself as flat as he could against the ground. It was several moments before Jamie dared to look up again but when he did, he could see the warrior was staring straight at them but now the green light from its mask had faded. Jamie knew that it wasn't a human face that he was looking at.

Too scared to move, they continued to lie on the ground, the cold damp earth penetrating through their clothes. The bird settled back on to the warrior's shoulder and watched them silently with its beady eyes.

"What do we do now? We can't stay here all night," Fiona whispered.

"Well you could try and take a photo."

But just as Fiona focused the camera for a second time, the warrior stepped back from the cliff edge; its birdlike mask glinting in the dim evening light as it moved. All three froze as the warrior turned towards them but instead of attacking them, the warrior turned away and strode off up the path. The raven, perched on its shoulder, swayed with every step as the giant warrior slowly became a dwindling shadow among the trees.

They all breathed a sigh of relief. "We'd better follow it," Fiona announced as she stood up and shook off the leaves and earth. "It might lead us to Murphy."

Fiona, believing the warrior hadn't seem them, was the first to stride off after it, but she was careful to keep well hidden in the shadows of the trees. At first, even Fergo was intrigued by where the warrior was going, but as they continued to follow it along the path, he could see the chimney stacks of Murphy's house looming closer with every step.

"It must be nearly ten feet tall," Fiona guessed as they jogged along trying to keep it in sight. "It could be a man on stilts."

"Did you see its eyes, Fiona? They weren't human," Jamie muttered. He could not believe that Fiona still thought it was a flesh-and-blood person. He was beginning to wonder if it was such a good idea following this giant beastie along the suddenly deserted cliff path after all.

But they kept up with the warrior until it finally halted outside the iron gates of Murphy's mansion. The warrior put its hands on the iron rails but the gates were locked tightly with two heavy padlocks. It moved towards the hedge and swinging its lance in a great wide arc, with one single blow it shattered the branches of the hedge, scattering leaves and twigs across the ground in all directions. The lance fell from its hands and vibrated on the ground. The warrior bent down on one knee – it looked as though the blow had used all its strength. Slowly, it turned its masked face towards the three of them, but as they were deep in argument, no one noticed the warrior look their way.

"I'm not going any further...Murphy could be in there at this very moment," Fergo was saying while Fiona looked at him witheringly.

"You'd never make a good reporter," she declared flatly. "Not enough nerve."

"Shut up, Fiona," Jamie snapped.

By the time they had finished arguing the warrior had disappeared completely from sight. Fiona quickly turned around to check it wasn't creeping up behind them and then they all slowly edged up towards the hole it had made in the hedge.

"Why didn't Murphy give him a key to the gate?" Fiona whispered as Fergo and Jamie peered through the gaping hole. But they didn't answer for in front of them lay Murphy's vast green lawn and at the edge of that his imposing white house that looked as impenetrable as a castle.

Fiona peered through the hole in the hedge and then with a determined look on her face, she squeezed through the gap. "We've got to find out if that warrior is just a man in disguise," she said.

Jamie didn't answer as he followed her. He didn't think it was going to be that simple.

There was no sign of the warrior anywhere. The only noise they could hear was the evening breeze rustling through the trees around them as the house stood in darkness.

"Where's Fergo?" Fiona whispered to Jamie, turning around. But Fergo had stayed on the other side of the hedge, adamant he was not going any further.

"What about the dogs? Murphy's bound to have guard dogs – it said so on the sign!" he whispered to them through the hedge.

Fiona tutted at him and they carried on regardless, leaving Fergo nervously hopping from foot to foot.

"Come back," he hissed as loudly as he dared. He looked back along the path the way they had just come. The sun was sinking lower and dark shadows from the trees were starting to create ghostly shapes across the path. He was just convincing himself that he was better off staying where he was when he heard a bird screech in the trees. His heart started to pound loudly in his chest as horrible pictures flashed through his mind. Without glancing back, he sprinted through the hole oblivious to his long coat snagging on the branches as he ran after the others. "Och, this is the end. I'm going to die," he muttered to himself.

6
The Discovery

As Jamie and Fiona crept warily around the garden towards the rear of the house, the lights from an open ground-floor window shone out on to the grass.

"Look," Fiona said, pointing towards the driveway as Fergo finally caught up with them. He was puffing hard, more from nerves than exertion as Fiona pointed to the Range Rover and another car parked in the driveway.

"Where's the warrior?" Fergo asked but no one had seen it since it had smashed through the hedge.

Jamie was the first to cross the open lawn towards the white walls of the house. The other two followed close behind and, walking with their backs to the cool walls, they crept along until they were positioned under the ledge of the lighted window. Luckily, the curtains were open wide enough for them to peer over and what they saw were two men examining a strange mask, not unlike the one the warrior was wearing.

"What's going on?" Jamie asked Fiona who had the best view. She brought her camera up and looked through the lens. "It's hard to tell, but the room is filled with stuff, really odd things...masks and bits of broken armour and old shields and swords and things," she whispered as her camera shutter clicked recording everything in the room. Then she spotted the tattered white moth-eaten owl on the shelf.

"What on earth is that? It looks horrible. I hope that's not your owl," said Fiona pointing out the rather bedraggled owl to Jamie. But Jamie didn't say a word for when he spotted the owl his eyes were transfixed. It seemed to be staring straight back at him. It was then that the message rung through in his head turning his blood as cold as ice. "Find the Ebony Owl," he whispered to himself. It was as if he had broken a coded message. The warrior had shown him the way to it. For a moment he could not drag his gaze away.

"This was meant to happen. I was supposed to find that owl," he said turning to stare at the others, but they were more interested in watching Murphy who was holding a strange mask carved in the shape of a bird's skull up to the light.

At that moment, Murphy straightened and turned towards the window, as though he had heard a noise. Fergo choked and fell backwards on to the grass. He could hardly forget that face.

"Murphy's seen me!" he squeaked.

Instantly Fiona and Fergo dropped down below the windowsill dragging Jamie down with them. After a few seconds they realised they had not been spotted so they slowly peered back over, one by one. Fergo shivered violently, even in his big thick coat. Too scared to blink in case they were seen, they all held their breath as Murphy walked about the room. They listened hard to hear snippets of the conversation. The other man had a microscope and some test tubes into which he was putting scrapings of the metal from one of the masks. He was scratching his head quizzically.

"These tests can't be wrong, but it's not reacting like any metal I've ever known," the man stated frankly.

"And what about this owl?" Murphy asked as the man picked it up and looked closely into its eyes.

"Under the feathers there's a hard body, but it's the X-ray pictures of what's inside that's most interesting. Look, there's something inside the owl," the man said holding up the X-ray for Murphy to see. "It's a solid crystal of some sort, made of a carbon compound that has been used in its eyes as well. I thought it might be a diamond but the compounds are different."

"What do you mean?" Murphy demanded.

"What I am trying to say is that the masks and this owl are not made from a material ever found before on this earth," the man told him. "This is a very significant scientific discovery."

Murphy grabbed the owl from him, rubbing his hands over its body as he stared at its eyes intently. "You must keep quiet about this. If anyone gets to know that I found this here, I'll never get my marina built. There'll be archaeologists and scientists crawling all over the place. No, I'll take it all down to London on Saturday. Then we'll wait until the marina's built before we tell anyone about it," he said sniggering. "Could be worth a fortune this, you know." Then he looked at the owl and smiled broadly for it seemed that he was the only one to have witnessed the owl's hidden power. Maybe there was a way he could use it for himself.

Meanwhile outside, Fiona was taking as many photographs as she could. Finally she turned to the others and whispered, "C'mon, I've got the photos." All three began to back away from the window, but just as Fiona had stowed her camera safely in her bag things went drastically wrong. It happened so fast that Fergo had no time even to yell out before he was lifted off the ground and a hand was clamped over his mouth. He heard the snarl of a dog close to his legs and saw that the other two were pinned against the wall too frightened to move in case the doberman sprung at them.

"Who have we got here then?" their captor questioned. "We better get the guv'nor out here now."

But Murphy had already heard the commotion, and coming over to the window, he spotted three frightened white faces.

"Get them away from the window!" he yelled and disappeared, but there was no thought of escape: Murphy appeared before them in a matter of moments. His thick eyebrows had formed into a single angry line and his nostrils flared after every word he spoke.

"What is going on here? Who's this snooping about?" he yelled, grabbing Jamie by the lapels of his jacket.

"Leave my brother alone, you evil worm," Fiona shouted, kicking out with her feet. "You didn't think that man in that silly disguise was going to scare us away from here, did you?"

Murphy looked puzzled for a moment. "What are you talking about?" He grabbed Fergo's torch and shone it directly into his face making his eyes water.

"It's you!" he roared. "First you dent my car and now you are trying to break into my house!" His face was inches from Fergo's who could smell his stale breath and see the beads of perspiration on his forehead. "What's your name?" he demanded.

"Ah...my name's Hamish," Fergo replied hurriedly, "and I don't know anything about your car, sir."

Murphy shook him by the collar. "Don't lie to me," he yelled. "What's your real name?"

"It's Fergus Montgomerie," Fergo squeaked in terror.

Murphy then glanced towards Jamie and Fiona, who stood motionless as the torch was shone in each of their faces.

"Now I know who *you* are. You're Maggie Logan's kids! I thought you two would've had more sense than to keep company with the likes of him," he said pointing at Fergo, who hung suspended by his long coat, his feet dangling inches above the ground. "I've a good mind to call the police and have you all done for trespassing!"

He let go of Fergo who dropped to the ground like a sack of potatoes and just lay there. But Murphy turned his attention to the security guard.

"How much did they see?" he asked the guard who was trying hard to stop the snarling dog from biting Fergo.

Jamie was the one to answer. "We didn't see anything, Murph...er...sir..." His voice sounded thin and squeaky and finally it petered out completely under Murphy's menacing stare.

"That doesn't sound very convincing," he shouted. His face was so close that Jamie could even see the red lines in his eyeballs. Murphy then turned to the guard again. "How did they get into the grounds?" he asked, but the man shrugged. Then Murphy let out a deep thoughtful sigh and bent down to look through the window at what the children had seen in his room. He saw the owl and he turned on the children, his face very red. Fiona gripped Jamie who was thinking Murphy was about to explode with rage, while Fergo cowered at the back believing their time was up for sure.

But suddenly Murphy seemed to relax, he rubbed his hands through his slicked-back hair and stared straight at them. He moved over towards Fergo. "Now tell me what you really saw?" he demanded, as he bent down to pick a twig from Fergo's coat. He snapped it in two with one hand.

Fergo clutched at his throat. "We di...didnae see anything, Mr Murphy. The room was empty!"

"That's what I want to hear but if I hear you saying otherwise, I'll 'ave you charged with criminal damage as well as trespass."

He pushed Fergo away and turned his attention to Fiona and Jamie. Fiona stepped back, clutching her bag with the camera behind her back, hoping they hadn't seen it.

"And as for you two," Murphy was saying, "you've got even more to lose than your friend here. Your mother's lease is up soon on that little café she runs on the seafront, isn't it? Now that's a prime spot. A good place for my new supermarket, that is. I don't think your mum would be suited to stacking shelves all day long, now would she?"

Fiona gasped. "You can't do that. The café is all our mum's got!"

"Then it's up to you to see that she keeps it. You three keep your mouths shut or else you'll be out on the streets."

All three of them just stared in shocked silence as he then ordered the guard to take them away.

"If I hear you've said a word to anyone about this," he yelled after them, "just remember I can change your lives...for the worst. Now get out of 'ere and don't come back!"

They were frogmarched out to the gate by the guard and his dog while Murphy stood and watched. When the guard came back Murphy stamped his feet and gave a disgruntled sigh. "I had to let 'em go. I can't have the police interfering, not while I have this stuff 'ere." He shook his head gravely and then his eyes narrowed. "How did they get through the front gates anyway?" he asked the guard.

"I've got no idea, Guv."

"Well find out!" Murphy screamed. "And if you let anyone else in 'ere you'll be down that road as fast as they are."

As soon as the iron gates had clanged shut behind them, the three of them sped off down the now darkened cliff path, not stopping until they were safely back to the well lit road. Any fears they'd had about the ghostly warrior were long forgotten, since being murdered by Murphy now seemed much more likely.

Finally, they all fell gasping on to the beach. Jamie could barely hear the waves crashing against the rocks as his breathing was so loud.

"I'd rather meet an army of ghostly beasties than go back up there," he heard Fergo say. "At least we can tell Angus that it's not a ghost after all, just Murphy up to no good."

"No, we can't. We can't tell a soul about what happened tonight," howled Fiona. "Murphy meant what he said. We can't let him take the café away!"

"But Fiona, Murphy isn't meant to have the owl. The warrior showed us the way and now it's up to me to get it out of there," Jamie said under his breath.

Fiona and Fergo turned to stare at him.

"Forget about the owl, Jamie, or we'll be in even more trouble than we're in now," Fiona said, and with that she and Fergo strode off.

Jamie had to run to catch up with them but they weren't going to listen to him.

"Fiona's right. We never saw the warrior again, not after it disappeared into the hedge," Fergo remarked.

"Yeh, I reckon he's just one of Murphy's thugs doing his job making sure no one sees what's going on in that house," Fiona replied.

"But what about the dreams, or those footsteps I saw in the sand? Murphy would have to be a magician to conjure those things up!" Jamie demanded. "You remember Fergo, you saw it, you were there."

But Fergo wasn't so sure. "But *they* can't harm us. Murphy can."

"See, Fergo doesn't even believe you. You could be making it all up. Making sure Mum keeps the café is more important than playing out your silly dreams." Fiona was angry. It was against her reporter's nature to have to keep quiet, but Murphy's threat had scared her.

"Well, Fiona, if it's proof you want, maybe your photos might help us," Jamie said. "They may give us something to go on."

"He'd kill us if he knew you had taken them," Fergo whispered as he looked back anxiously at the cliffs and pulled the collar of his coat up around his ears. Above them a flock of crows were circling the trees and cawing out into the night.

Jamie hung back for the birds seemed to be peering down at him, watching him closely. He felt sure that they were up against more than just Murphy.

7
The Battle

Fiona wanted to get the film developed as quickly as possible in case the prints were evidence against Murphy. But Jamie just wanted to see the owl again for himself. They pooled their money together and took the film to the chemist to be developed early the next morning. They hung around the amusement arcade waiting for the hour to be up before they went back to collect the prints. However when they arrived, they could tell from the expression on the technician's face that something was wrong.

"I have never seen anything like this happen to a black and white film before," the girl said. Jamie turned to look at Fiona's disappointed face and his heart sank. After all the risk, something was wrong with the photographs.

"Was it too dark? I'm sure I used all the right settings,"

Fiona asked trying to peek at the prints the girl was flicking through.

Even from that distance she could tell that every single picture was filled with shards of emerald green light. Once she handed them over, they could all see that the light became brighter and brighter until finally, on the very last photo, it overpowered everything else.

Fiona looked baffled as they had seen nothing like that through Murphy's window. But then, when she looked again, the source of the luminous light suddenly became clear. Jamie also spotted it and he gasped out loud.

"I don't understand it," the technician kept saying, scratching her head and turning the photograph on its side. "What is this photograph of anyway?" she asked.

Fiona became decidedly nervous "Och...it's only a cheap camera, it probably let some light in. I shouldn't bother worrying," she said as she whipped the prints out of the girl's hands before any more questions could be asked. "How much do we owe?"

The technician stared at them blankly as Fiona pushed the money at her and dashed for the door, the two boys close behind. Outside, no one could wait to see the photographs again. They hurriedly pulled all the prints from the envelope. It was obvious that the light was coming straight from the old stuffed owl's eyes.

"See, I told you it wasn't an ordinary owl!" Jamie exclaimed happily. Now they had to believe him.

"Its eyes look like two traffic lights on 'go'," Fergo remarked.

"Well, it didn't look like that last night," said Fiona. "It just sat there like an old tatty stuffed bird."

Jamie was staring intently at one of the photographs. The emerald green eyes seemed to become even brighter the more he looked at it. Once again the voice echoed through his head. "Find the owl," he said out loud. "This is the owl I was told to find," he said.

Fergo took the photo away from him and stared at it. "But it's Murphy's...Those jewel eyes are probably worth thousands, he's hardly going to hand them over to you!"

"But I think they're more than just jewels!" Jamie exclaimed. "They are the magical eyes of the Ebony Owl." He could feel his face turning red as the others stared at him in disbelief.

"Oh, Jamie, how do you know that?" Fiona asked. "Anyway, shouldn't an Ebony Owl be black? This one's white and feathery with green eyes!"

Jamie couldn't explain but he knew he was right. "I just know it's the Ebony Owl...I just know it is." Jamie declared defiantly.

They met in their mum's café early the next day. Fiona was helping to make up sandwiches for the lunchtime rush, while Jamie and Fergo sat despondently at the back eating crusts of bread as they tried to figure out what to do about Murphy.

"Maybe we should tell the police and give them the photographs," Fergo suggested as Fiona brought them over some freshly made baps.

"And tell them what?" asked Fiona. "That we've been trespassing. We've no proof he's doing anything illegal and anyway even if we did have, we can't go near the police. Fergo you could be arrested and you know what he said he would do to our café."

"Even if we did get him put in jail, Murphy would probably send someone else to kill us," Fergo whispered.

"We need to find out about the owl," said Jamie.

Both Fiona and Fergo turned to stare at him. "Oh, just forget about that stupid owl, Jamie!" Fergo snapped angrily.

Even Fiona just stared at Jamie witheringly. "And what are you going to do?" she asked. "You can't just walk up to Murphy now and ask him what he knows about owls with bright green eyes."

Jamie shrugged his shoulders. "I'll think of something."

"Well, I'm off," Fergo said as he got up and walked past him. "I've had enough of that stupid old scruffy owl."

Fiona went back to help her mum behind the counter, leaving Jamie staring out of the door after Fergo. He glared back at his sister and, for a moment, he wished that he had never laid eyes on the owl. But he knew that he was somehow linked to it. But Fiona was right, he didn't have a clue what he was going to do next.

That night Jamie took the photos to bed with him. He could hardly bear to put them down and his mind kept racing over the words: "Find the Ebony Owl...Find the owl." But even if he managed to get it away from

Murphy, what was he supposed to do with it? He put his head under his pillow, the photographs clenched tightly in his hand. As he finally fell asleep he didn't see the owl's bright green eyes shining out like a beacon across his bedroom. In the middle of the night, the wind rose from the sea and battered the houses along the seafront. Jamie woke up once when the wind blew leaves and twigs against his bedroom window and then, his head back on the pillow, he drifted into a deep slumber only to have the dream begin the minute his eyes closed.

At first he had thought it was just the beating of his heart, but then he realised that it was a distant drumbeat and he was standing above the battlefield looking down into the valley. In the far north the advancing army marched towards him, their mighty owl banners flying majestically above their heads. They were soon close enough for Jamie to hear the clink of their armour and see that this army was made up of rank after rank of great warrior birdmen. There seemed to be no stopping their advance until from behind, Jamie heard the familiar voices of shouting men. He turned to see another army approaching. Seconds later the two sides clashed and the battle was underway. Soon the air was filled with the sounds of war; the pounding of clubs and swords and the cries of falling men filled his ears. The battle seemed endless, but Jamie realised that it was the tall warrior birdmen who were gaining ground. These strange masked warriors were slaying the smaller army of men who did not have a chance against their mighty weapons which were made of a stronger metal, able to slice through the lesser weapons like knives through butter.

Soon, the birdmen were so advanced that their line of command could be seen at the back, watching the battle from the safety of the hills. Jamie's eyes narrowed surveying each one until he saw something that made him stop. The sounds of battle forgotten, Jamie eyes were focused on only one thing, for there on a high podium, sat a shiny black owl with the brightest green eyes that Jamie had ever seen.

Then Jamie was distracted by shouts from behind him. He turned to see on the hill, a group of people huddled together over large black cauldrons that hung over three roaring fires. In his dream, he was there in a second, now well behind the front line of attack, completely unnoticed by anyone in the chaos of this dream. Then he saw a boy who, though slightly older, bore a remarkable resemblance to himself. Jamie ran to him, but at that moment the boy was called over to the middle cauldron. Around this fire, the oldest of the men sat. Cloaked in dark stained robes they poured over the pages of thick books, each person seemingly performing a different task, either reading, or measuring out brightly-coloured powders which were flung into the big black cauldron. The smell was appalling and Jamie held his hands over his face as he watched them work. He could sense it was a time of great magic and that some awesome spell was being prepared in order to try and stop the advancing army.

Finally, with the enemy warriors nearly upon them, Jamie watched as from each of the other cauldrons a portion of the mixture was added. Jamie could not help but gasp when the boy produced the pendant which hung on a leather thong around his neck. He took it off and threw it into the cauldron causing the liquid to explode into a boiling froth. By now all the sorcerers were gathered, and chanting together they forced their spell out over the landscape. Instantly the whole field became covered in a dense blue smoke. Then they began to hear the yells from the other army. Soon these yells turned into birdlike calls and as Jamie watched, the birdmen were falling helplessly to the ground. But only their robes were landing in heaps, as from the sleeves and necks of their tunics, birds had begun to appear. They were being transformed in front of him. These birds then flew up into the sky, circled, and disappeared. The battle had ended. The mighty spell had worked and the enemy warriors had been transformed into harmless birds. The mist began to clear and it was then that Jamie saw the great podium swaying with the owl balanced precariously on the top. The spell was still working and he watched amazed as finally the owl toppled to the ground and disappeared into the rolling mist. Jamie followed the boy who was sent out to search for the lost owl but it had vanished, so deeply cloaked was it in magic.

At this point, the dream faded and Jamie found himself back in his own room again but it was as if he had been running and was out of breath. He stared up at the ceiling, picturing the boy's face and the familiar pendant worn around his neck. Was that his dad's pendant – the same pendant that had won the battle against the army of birdmen? But now he had the pendant and after all this time its magic had suddenly come to life. Was it about to be needed again? He glanced down at the owl in the photograph and wondered what was going to happen next.

8
The Professor

The next day, without telling the others, Jamie went off on his own to think things through. He wasn't paying much attention to where he was going so it was with some surprise that he found himself in the centre of the town. Playing with the pendant in his pocket, he wandered on through the crowd before turning up the street that led to the school at the top of the hill. As he wandered up, his gaze caught on something in a window of a shop that made him stop. A stuffed owl was staring straight at him from inside the shop window. For one incredible moment Jamie thought it was the Ebony Owl and he froze where he stood, but then a car beeped its horn at him and he realised he had stopped right in the middle of the road. He took a few steps towards the shop and surveyed the wrought iron sign swinging in the breeze above the door. It squeaked in the wind as he read it:

Professor Mungo Moncrieff –
Curios, Antiquities,
and things Supernatural

Jamie walked over to the front of the shop where an 'OPEN' sign hung in the window, but pressing his face against the glass, he could not see anyone inside. He turned the handle of the door and the bell tinkled so loudly that whoever was inside now knew that he was there. Jamie walked on into the dark interior of the old and dimly lit shop.

As his eyes slowly adjusted to the light, Jamie saw that on the left hand side the wall was lined with bookshelves, crammed so tightly with books that it was hard to see where one ended and the next began. Jamie went over to read a few of the dusty spines and they all seemed to be about mythology and astrology. On the walls above him hung great charts of hieroglyphics and other odd symbols, while beneath these, on wooden shelves, were bottles and jars filled with coloured powders and potions. Jamie moved slowly around the shelves until he came to a glass case full of old stuffed birds and animals. Jamie stared hard at the birds but their eyes were just made of lifeless black glass. A sparrow hawk and a barn owl stared back at him, but there was nothing that resembled the mysterious green-eyed owl.

All this time Jamie had not sensed the presence of anyone else. Then he saw a curtain move and, from among the bookshelves at the back, a small man stepped forward. He gave Jamie a warm, friendly smile, and held out his hand in welcome.

"I'm Professor Mungo Moncrieff. May I be of help?" the old man said, holding on to Jamie's hand.

Jamie was too surprised by the appearance of the Professor to notice at first how intently he was being stared at. He was an elderly man with long flowing grey hair and a beaky nose and round stooped shoulders. He wore dark green plaid trousers, and a green cardigan that hung like limp wings around his body. On his yellow waistcoat was a gold chain.

Jamie smiled back briefly. "I'm here about an..." Jamie stopped suddenly. The Professor continued to stare at him but Jamie could not bring himself to speak.

"A book on astrology for your mother perhaps?" the Professor asked pointing to his books and charts.

"No," Jamie replied firmly. He decided he had nothing to lose in telling the Professor a little about the owl. "I need to find out some information about an...owl."

"Well, you've come to the right place. I know a little about ornithology, but my field of expertise lies more in the study of ancient civilisations, both real and mythical," he said. "So I might be able to help you. What sort of owl are you interested in?"

Jamie dragged his gaze away from the Professor to look up at the stuffed birds and animals. They looked harmless compared to the Ebony Owl. What would it hurt to show the Professor the photograph of the Ebony Owl? He felt for the photograph in his pocket and fingered it nervously trying to decide what he should say.

"It's just one owl I'm interested in. It's an Ebony Owl with bright green eyes." Then he took the photograph from this pocket. "Would you know anything about an owl like this one?" he asked hopefully handing him the photograph.

The Professor looked at it. "You say it's an owl made of ebony?"

Jamie nodded as the Professor rubbed his chin, deep in thought. "There was a story I once heard...now what was it?" he asked himself looking hard at the photograph again. Then he shook his head and peered at Jamie over the rim of his glasses.

"How did it come to be in your possession?" he asked.

"It's not mine," Jamie replied, "but I think it's important that I find out who it really belongs to."

"Indeed! It is quite magnificent and somehow I don't believe this is an ordinary stuffed bird," the Professor stated. "Tell me all you know, then maybe I will remember something else."

The Professor was so interested that Jamie felt he could tell him the whole story, right from the start when Angus had first seen the warrior. The Professor was so intent on the details that Jamie found himself telling him about his dreams, which was something only Fiona and Fergo vaguely knew about, but instead of laughing like the others, the Professor did not interrupt him once.

"Let me see the photograph again," was all he asked

when finally Jamie ran out of words. He stared at it with a magnifying glass and glanced back at Jamie. All the time Jamie had been speaking, the Professor had been making notes. Now he flipped the pages over as he spoke. "Your story is most fascinating. I now recall hearing a story about a Scottish legend of an ancient people who worshipped an enchanted owl, but there has never been any evidence found of its existence. I believe I may have some papers on it somewhere but it will take a little time to collect them. If you were to give me your address," he said, "I will be in touch."

He held out a pen to Jamie who took it. He glanced up at the Professor, wondering if he was doing the right thing, but as no one else seemed able to help he had little choice. He wrote down the details on the back of the photograph. The Professor took it from him, thanked him briefly, and then disappeared behind the curtain at the back of his shop without another word.

For a few moments Jamie hung around wondering if the Professor would come back. But when he didn't, he edged his way nervously towards the door of the old dusty shop, anxious to be outside in the fresh air.

It was only after Jamie had gone that the Professor appeared again. He moved quickly to the window to watch Jamie walking away down the street.

"What is your link with an owl like this, young Jamie Logan?" the Professor said to himself as he stared at the boy's scribbled name and address.

9
Facts Unearthed

For the next few days, Jamie wondered if the Professor would get in touch but no word came. What would he do if the Professor was unable to help him after all? For some reason Jamie felt time was running out. Ever since the night up at Murphy's house strange things had happened. Work had again been interrupted at Murphy's marina after a small flock of cormorants had flown in to roost on the cliffs right above the area Murphy was excavating. Flocks of rare sea birds, not normally seen in those parts, had also been spotted coasting in towards Craiginver on the sea breezes to land on any rock or nook and cranny they could find on the cliffs. In parts of the harbour every branch or ledge was now filled with the sound of loudly screeching birds. Members of ornithological societies from all over the country had been called in to study their strange behaviour.

Meanwhile the locals were also in danger from the normally peaceful seagulls who had now started to attack anyone who stopped on the pier. No one was safe to eat their fish suppers outdoors any more.

But though Jamie knew the strange bird activity was linked to the sudden appearance of the mysterious owl, he was more worried that the Professor would not be able to help him. He had tried the shop's telephone number many times but there had been no answer.

One afternoon, with the rain falling outside, Jamie was sitting despondently at the kitchen table looking hard at the owl in the photograph. He heard Fergo come pounding around the side of the house but didn't bother getting out of his chair.

"What are you doing moping around here?" his friend asked. "I thought we were going down to the arcade."

"I was hoping the Professor would call, but he hasn't. Doesn't look like he's been able to find anything," Jamie replied, sighing loudly.

They were still talking about it when they heard a knock at the front door. Jamie stood up and stared at the door. Only strangers knocked at the front door.

"Maybe it's Murphy!" Fergo squeaked. They both held their breath hoping whoever it was would go away, but the knocking continued. They crept into the front room and Jamie peered through a slit in the curtains. There was nothing much to see except sheets of heavy rain, but then Jamie glimpsed a figure huddling in the porch.

"It's the Professor," he cried.

Fergo came up and glanced through the curtain behind him. The Professor spotted the movement in the curtain and waved.

"He's half drowned," Fergo commented.

Jamie dropped the curtain hurriedly as the Professor began to rap even harder on the door. Jamie opened the door to the small bedraggled man. His overcoat was wet through but he did not seem at all bothered by the downpour.

"Hello, Jamie, I've got to talk to you," the Professor said shaking his hand. His face was lit with a warm and inquisitive smile. "I may have found something," he said. It was only then that the Professor turned to see Fergo.

"And are you one of Jamie's friends?" he asked. "My name is Professor Moncrieff. Who are you?"

"I'm Fergus Montgomerie; Jamie's best friend," Fergo replied, looking up warily at the Professor's outstretched arm.

"Well, do you think I might come in out of this rain?" asked the Professor smiling.

Jamie stepped back as the drenched Professor walked into the hallway, dripping water all over the carpet. For several moments Fergo just stood in front of the Professor staring at him as a puddle of water grew on the carpet.

Finally, Jamie realised the Professor was waiting and he led him past Fergo through to the bright warm kitchen.

Without saying a word he took the Professor's waterlogged overcoat from him. Underneath the overcoat the Professor was clutching a satchel to his chest to keep it dry. He made his way towards the kitchen table where he drew up a chair and sat down. He then drew out eight fragile pages of parchment from the satchel, smiling at Jamie as he did so. He began to arrange them carefully on the table.

"What do you think of these?" he asked Jamie. "Look closely and you will see that pictures of an owl feature on some of the pages, an owl not unlike the one in your photograph. Several pages are missing but I think the pictures may show enough for us to piece a few of the facts together."

Jamie looked at the strange pictures and symbols on the pieces of parchment and though he could see the outline of an owl as the Professor said, he could make no sense of the words.

"Now what we need is some sort of key to unlock these secrets," the Professor said pointing to the lines of text, but Jamie could not make head nor tail of the strange symbols. He looked up at the Professor who, disappointed, gave a deep sigh.

"Is there anything from your dream that comes to mind? Anything at all?" he asked.

Then Jamie had a thought. It was a long shot, but it was the only thing he could think of. "Maybe my dad's pendant could help us," he said producing the pendant from his pocket.

"But that's just your dad's lucky charm. It's been sitting

on your shelf for years. There's nothing magical about that," Fergo said butting in.

"Maybe not then, but since the day that raven attacked me it has changed," Jamie replied. He began to rub the centre of it and the dull metal glimmered and then slowly, it began to spin. Fergo gasped as Jamie placed it on the table. "I remember Dad telling me that someday I might need it. He told me that it had always brought luck to the Logan family but that its real power had never been needed. I thought he was just making it up...that it was just a story; but now, maybe...maybe he was right."

Taking a chance Jamie held the pendant above one of the parchments and, suddenly, the shapes and the misshapen letters changed. The small intricate pictures became clearer while the text formed itself into neat concise lines. Jamie looked up at the Professor who was pouring over the pages in amazement as the magic from the pendant began to slowly unravel the story. Hurriedly, the Professor spread each of the fragile sheets out on the table. Fergo gasped and pointed, for he could see that one picture now clearly depicted the owl with bright gleaming green eyes.

"That, without a doubt, is the same owl that you showed me," the Professor said incredulously.

"But where did you find these papers?" Jamie asked him cautiously.

"For years I've collected stories and documents about legendary and supernatural places," he said. "But these pages have always been a mystery. Until, that is, the day you showed up at my door. Somehow I knew you were linked to this story."

He then pulled a notebook from his satchel and compared his own notes to the text written before him. "Now give me a moment while I study these," he said, and with that he began to scan the text on the first page.

"Well, this looks like an ancient Celtic language. Many of these words I think I can decipher," he said finally.

He then pointed out to Jamie another picture of the owl but this time at its feet lay a white egg, the size of a fist. Jamie noticed that the owl sat on a tall podium and beneath it a group of birdlike warriors stood with their heads bowed in worship. The warriors looked just like the one they had seen on the cliffs.

"That's our warrior!" Jamie exclaimed to Fergo as he pointed to the picture.

"Another reason to believe these parchments hold the answer," the Professor replied, but then his smile died as he read a passage again. He began to flick furiously through the pages of his notebook. "It seems that this owl may be more important than you imagined." He glanced cautiously at Jamie.

"What's wrong?" Fergo asked.

"Well, it seems that this owl was a sacred idol worshipped by the people from a place called Fengall, but it was lost to them many, many, centuries ago," the Professor said, his round eyes glancing piercingly up at

Jamie. "From what I gather it was lost during a great battle that took place around these parts. Now it seems that owl has turned up at last. The sighting of the lone warrior on the cliffs could be a sign that not only do the Fengall people exist, but also that they know the Ebony Owl has been unearthed here. If only one warrior was sent then maybe their strength and magical skills are weak now. I think time is running out for them all."

"But why is this owl so important to them?" Fergo asked.

The Professor flicked back to the picture of the owl and his finger traced a shape around the white egg. He frowned deeply and then his eyes opened wider and his mouth fell open.

"My goodness...they may have come in time for the egg."

"What do you mean, Professor?" Fergo asked.

"The Ebony Owl lays a precious egg once every 2,000 years. This egg is made from a rare crystal that provides the Fengalls with the life source they need to keep their warrior-like form. But without the owl and its crystal egg, their power has grown so weak that soon all the remaining Fengall warriors will revert back to their birdlike shape, forced to live in the trees without the ability to walk or speak ever again. The only way to save their remaining numbers is for the Ebony Owl to be returned to Fengall in time for the laying of the new crystal."

"Where is this place called Fengall?" Fergo asked.

The Professor glanced towards Jamie. "I think Jamie

may know something about that," he said and Jamie felt his heart give a lurch. "You didn't come across this owl by chance, did you?"

Jamie shivered but said nothing.

"Is this true? Did you know about this all along?" Fergo asked, his mouth hanging open.

"No, but when I saw the owl for the first time, I knew I had seen it in a dream," said Jamie.

"Well, Jamie, the story shows that it could have been an ancestor of yours, some great magician, who cast the spell that banished the people of Fengall from our world. And though you may not know it yet, you have some of that power within you. Used with the pendant your power may be a very important gift."

Then the Professor turned another page and Jamie's eyes were drawn to the picture of a boy, the boy from his dream walking across a battlefield. Around his neck, on a leather thong, was the star-shaped pendant!

"He does look like you a bit," Fergo remarked but then noticed that the Professor's attention had turned to the next page.

"What's the matter?" Fergo asked, while Jamie glanced nervously at the Professor whose fingers were tracing the words hurriedly, his mouth moving silently as he tried to decipher each new line.

"If I am right and they are seeking the egg, then it may mean that it is about to be laid. The Ebony Owl must be returned very soon," the Professor stated.

For a moment neither boy said a word.

"But where should it be returned to?" Jamie managed at last.

"To Fengall," the Professor replied. "And it seems that you are the one who must do this."

"*Jamie,* to take the owl back to Fengall?" Fergo gasped in amazement, but his question was ignored as Jamie and the Professor stared hard at each other.

"Jamie, the unearthing of this Ebony Owl has unleashed a strange force in this village. If the Ebony Owl is not put back in its rightful place who knows what will happen. It may be impossible to ignore now, no matter how hard you try."

Jamie stayed silent. He felt shocked at the Professor's words but it all seemed to make sense. His dreams were suddenly becoming very real – the warrior sightings, the sudden empowering of his dad's pendant and then finally, the appearance of the mysterious Ebony Owl. Jamie fingered the scar on the palm of his hand. Maybe, if he was to return the owl, everything would go back to normal.

"But Jamie you haven't got the owl. It's up there inside that house. The house that we are never *ever* going back to," he heard Fergo remind him. "Have you forgotten what Murphy said would happen if he ever caught us up there? Your mum will lose the café and I might have to go to jail!"

Fergo could hardly believe his ears when Jamie, ignoring him, stood up and turned towards the Professor.

"Tonight may be the only chance. We heard Murphy

say he is taking the owl away to London tomorrow."

"Well then, once we have the owl safe, then we can try and piece together what must be done next," the Professor replied.

Jamie didn't get a chance to ask any more questions for the next moment there was a loud yell from the hallway. Fergo jumped nearly a foot in the air, as Fiona came in complaining about the puddles of water in the hall. The boys had forgotten to shut the door behind them.

"What on earth is going on?" she asked, spotting the wet and crumpled Professor perched on the edge of a kitchen chair as she came into the kitchen.

"This is Professor Moncrieff. He's here about Jamie's owl," Fergo replied.

"*Jamie's* owl! It's hardly Jamie's owl!" Fiona replied. Then as she turned to the strange-looking Professor, she got out her reporter's notebook. "So Jamie was right, it's not just an old stuffed bird then?" she asked.

"Of course not, but I don't know how much this person called Murphy realises yet. It is possible he only thinks its eyes are of value. I doubt that he has any knowledge of its true power."

The Professor showed Fiona the parchments and explained.

"But how did the owl end up here in the first place?" Fiona asked.

"It seems that in ancient times, somewhere very close to here a great battle between the Celts and the Fengalls took place," the Professor began as he showed her a page depicting the battle between the two great armies.

"I've seen that!" Jamie cried pointing to the picture which showed a group of warriors with a banner of a large black owl. He retold the story. "I saw what happened. The Fengall army was so strong and many Celts were dying," Jamie began. "The only way to stop them was to bring every sorcerer and magician to the battlefield to cast a powerful spell on the Fengall idol, the Ebony Owl, in the hope that it would end the battle," he remarked.

"Jamie, how do you know this?" Fiona asked.

Jamie shrugged his shoulders. "In my dream I was there on the battlefield," he said shyly.

The Professor, reading on as fast as he could across the page, took up the story. "Jamie's right. The Celts bombarded the Fengalls with their spells and incantations. The barrage was so strong that not only was the owl toppled from the podium, but it had become so tightly cloaked in magic it was lost. However, they succeeded in defeating the Fengall force and that was all that mattered."

"And the owl was never seen again?" Fergo asked.

"Until now that is. It seems that over the centuries the legend has been forgotten. But now the Ebony Owl has been uncovered here in this village and, because of the warrior on the cliffs, we know that the Fengalls have come back for it."

"But why do they need me?" Jamie asked.

"It seems what your ancestors started, you must finish. There is a gateway that leads from here into Fengall. That must still be shrouded in a strong spell that only you can break. Once that is done, then the two worlds would be linked and the Ebony Owl could pass back through into its own world." The three looked at the Professor in silence. "This page even shows the gateway through to Fengall." The Professor pointed to the next pages which showed an archway standing high and alone on a great deserted moor.

The Professor glanced at his watch. "However, Jamie, if what you say is true about Murphy taking the owl away, then we must act now."

Jamie realised that he was gripping the pendant tightly. He didn't know what to do? Could he trust the Professor or was it some kind of trap? He glanced up at the old man who was gathering his papers together. At that moment the pendant suddenly became very warm in his hand. Was this a sign that he was meant to go? He would have to take the chance.

Meanwhile Fiona and Fergo were staring speechlessly at each other as Jamie stood up from the table. Neither could believe how Jamie had become involved in all this but they followed him out to the back porch where he put on his anorak.

"What about Murphy? Even if you do manage to get the owl, he'll soon notice that it's gone," Fiona said.

"I've already thought about that," the Professor replied. "We'll stop off at my shop on the way, Jamie." And with that he ushered Jamie out, gripping his satchel as he headed for the door eagerly.

Fergo and Fiona watched as they disappeared with their heads down and bodies bent against the force of the driving rain. For a moment Fergo and Fiona just stood in the doorway.

"We can't just let Jamie go up there on his own with that old man," Fiona said finally turning to grab her coat and hurrying to put it on. "C'mon Fergo, we might as well find out what's so special about this owl – *and* about my little brother."

Fergo grumbled, but when Fiona took his hand he went willingly. The two of them had to run hard to catch up with Jamie and the Professor who were marching boldly off into the wind and rain. Waves crashed over the sea wall on to the pavement but the old Professor seemed undeterred by this and marched on purposefully with Jamie following close behind.

"Don't worry Fergo, we'll die of pneumonia before Murphy has a chance to get his hands on us," Fiona said squeezing Fergo's hand. Fergo glanced up at her and managed a smile.

10
Breaking In

The light was grey and a little dim when the Professor finally unlocked the door to his shop. He turned on the lights and then picked up the stuffed barn owl from the top shelf. Its feathers were nearly as white as Fengall's Ebony Owl, but its eyes were brown and made of glass. He picked it up and gave it to Fergo to carry, then he handed Fiona a metal toolbox. Locking up the shop, the little party continued on along the waterfront and up on to the cliff path.

They met no one on the way up the path, and although they all kept a watchful eye, the warrior did not appear.

Finally they reached the hedge surrounding Murphy's property. There were no cars or trucks in the driveway and Fergo whispered to the Professor that he had seen Murphy's car driving out of the village earlier. The

Professor rattled the strong metal chains on the gate while Jamie wandered about poking in the hedge, until he found the gap where he knew the branches were broken. Once on the other side, the professor pulled the branches back together again, concealing the hole as best he could.

They were all thankful that the rain gave them good cover as, bent over, they ran on towards the house. Luckily, no one seemed aware of their intrusion.

"This is where we saw the owl the last time," Jamie said as he lead the Professor up to the window.

They peered into the dark room. At first they thought someone had left a small oil lamp burning on the bench, but when they brushed the window with their sleeves to get a better view, they could see the light was coming from the owl which lay cradled in its metal box, staring up at the ceiling with its eyes glowing dimly. Fergo produced his torch and shone it through into the room and they all pressed their faces up against the glass.

"It's hard to see anything in there," Fiona declared, but then as though it heard her words, the owl's eyes began to glow more brightly.

"Agh, I'm going. This is too creepy!" hissed Fergo but Fiona clamped a hand over his mouth before he could say another word.

"For goodness sake keep quiet."

"But what are we going to do?" Fergo enquired.

The Professor and Jamie looked at each other and Jamie nodded. "I'll go in and get it," he said, and with that he pulled on the window, but it was securely locked.

"Here, let me try," the Professor offered. He pulled a small chisel from the toolbox with which he worked at the window until there was a gap in the frame. He pushed at it until finally the window opened. They pulled it upwards with only a slight squeak. Fergo and Fiona moved back and stared around the grounds hoping that Murphy would not arrive back and catch them.

"Now, Jamie, be careful, there could be an alarm," the Professor told him as he handed him the toolbox and the fake owl. Jamie took them, nodded and then clambered through the window.

He dropped into the room and lay flat on his stomach, holding his breath in case he should set off an alarm. Luckily, nothing happened and so, trying hard not to shake, he began to crawl across the floor. Halfway across, he turned to look back at Fiona and Fergo and he could just make out their white faces staring at him.

"Keep going, Jamie, it's not far now," Fergo whispered.

"Yeh, then we can all go home," Fiona shivered and grabbed hold of Fergo's coat wishing her brother would hurry up. Jamie had never done anything like this in his life before and she had deep misgivings about having ever let him leave the warmth and comfort of their house in the first place. But Jamie was so adamant about this. He had never said much about his dreams, but she had heard how his nights had been tormented, sometimes making him cry out in fear. She knew that nothing she could have said or done would change his mind. All she could do was stand and watch as her little brother crept across the floor of Murphy's house.

Inside, Jamie was trying hard to remain calm. He found it hard to breathe. The air was stuffy as though all the oxygen had been used up. It was also very dark, save for the dim light given out by the eyes of the owl which sat on the other side of the room. He stood up and immediately tripped over the leg of a chair. He was sent sprawling, while the chair screeched across the floor. Outside, three heads ducked beneath the window as everyone held their breath waiting to see what would happen. But the house remained quiet. Jamie took a deep breath and carefully walking on tiptoes this time, he crept on towards the owl.

"Be careful, Jamie," the Professor whispered from the window but at that moment it seemed as though all the lights in the room came on by themselves. Jamie wheeled around towards the doorway to see who had turned them on, only to discover that the room was being illuminated by the light from the owl's eyes. Their brilliance was so strong, that the room was suddenly lit from wall to wall.

Jamie swallowed hard. He had to shield his eyes against the brightness and as he moved closer, his jaw dropped open as he realised that the owl had switched its gaze and was staring straight back at him. Jamie felt the pull from its eyes as though he was being drawn in towards their very centre. It took all his strength to reach into his pocket for the pendant. He pulled it out and placed it in front of his face. The green light intensified and Jamie felt the heat through the pendant, but then it died away. Now Jamie could look directly at the owl. He could see that its motley white feathers were burnt and singed, as though it was burning from the inside out, and underneath the layer of feathers he could just make out a black shiny body.

"It *is* made of ebony," he gasped while outside he could hear Fergo's frantic whisper. "Someone's coming!"

For a moment Jamie froze, panic overriding everything else before he realised that if he turned back now, there would be no other chance.

Although he could hardly believe what he was doing, he moved forward until he was so close to the owl he could smell the charring feathers and feel the heat from its body. All he had to do was pick up the owl and replace it with the Professor's, put the lid down and then escape but at this point his courage nearly deserted him. His hands were shaking so much he could barely open the lid of the Professor's toolbox. He fumbled and the metal case fell to the floor with a loud clang. He scrambled frantically to retrieve it.

"Hurry, Jamie!" he heard Fiona call.

Jamie was now numb with fear, but he managed to pick up the Ebony Owl in his shaking hands and put it into the Professor's case. He then placed the fake owl in the Fengall case and shut both lids. Instantly, all light was extinguished and he had to pick his way back across the room, trying to avoid hitting the furniture on the way. He could hear the others calling to him, but he could go no faster as there were so many obstacles in his way. He made it back to the window and handed the owl through to Fergo who held the toolbox gingerly before dropping it on the ground when he felt the heat radiating off the metal handle. The toolbox opened and the owl rolled out on the grass revealing its warm body to the others for the first time.

"Don't look at it," Jamie hissed in warning as he tried to squeeze back through the window, but all three of them immediately moved forward for a closer look at the owl.

"It's steaming hot!" Fergo yelled jumping backwards in fright.

"Be quiet, Fergo!" snapped Fiona, as she went to help her brother out of the window.

"I can't believe we have just done this!" she said to him but when she turned she could feel herself being magnetically pulled towards the owl whose eyes were now glowing very brightly.

Quickly, Jamie placed the pendant into Fiona's palm. He made her hold it in front of her face as she looked down at the owl. Even with the pendant she could still feel its powers pulling her. But then the pendant began to repel the owl's intense magical powers. Jamie quickly made Fergo do the same, but it was too late for the Professor who was caught directly in their beam.

"Professor, don't look at it," he pleaded but the Professor was unable to look away from the owl's eyes. He was drawn forward towards the owl, his fingertips lightly grazing the owl's body. In that instant, the owl's eyes locked fiercely on to his own. He had never dreamed that its power would be so great. Jamie tugged at the Professor's coat but all he could do was watch helplessly as the Professor's eyes grew darker and his face took on a strange look. For a second his breathing stopped. Jamie called to Fergo to help him and together they knocked the Professor to the ground, prizing him away from the owl which rolled face down on to the grass. Fergo bent over the prone Professor. He could see his pupils were like round black holes filling the whole iris. He had been completely overwhelmed by the owl's power.

"Murphy had that same look the day I saw him at the harbour," Fergo said shivering.

Fiona, standing back in the rain, kept a watch on the owl as the remainder of the white feathers became matted as raindrops hit its warm body. Small puffs of steam hissed into the air with every drop.

"C'mon, we have to get out of here," she said as Jamie picked up the owl, placing it into the box. He shut the lid, instantly extinguishing the light, but the damage had already been done.

Jamie stared at the Professor who had finally come round. His pupils were still large and fixed, and he was breathless and pale. Then they heard a door slam and loud voices coming towards them through the darkened house. They had to get away quickly. Dragging the Professor, the four crept away from the window to hide in the shadows of the garden.

As they clambered back through the hedge and out on to the path, the rain stopped. They all let out a sigh of relief but then Fiona stopped in her tracks. She heard the loud screech of a bird. It sounded like the one they had heard the first night they had ventured on the cliff path; in fact it sounded a lot like the warrior's black raven.

"What was that?" Fiona shouted.

"Just the wind in the trees," the Professor replied distractedly. But Fiona stopped to listen and sure enough, at the top of a tree she could just make out the large shape of a bird watching them. At the base of the tree hidden in the shadows, she thought she saw an outline of a tall warrior-like figure but she could not be sure. When she blinked and looked again there was nothing to be seen.

She ran to catch up with the others and they walked together helping the Professor back down through the windswept trees. Fergo looked back anxiously at every second step in case they were being followed, but there was no sign of anyone. It was too wild an evening for walkers, or even Murphy to be about.

11
The Flight

With the owl safely in their possession, and hopefully Murphy not aware of his loss, they made their way back down towards the village. A storm had blown up and with every gust of wind, the rain lashed the seafront in a relentless torrent. No one noticed them pass and soon they were in the safety and warmth of the Professor's home above his shop. He sat down heavily in his armchair and Fiona rushed to get him a glass of water.

"Are you all right, Professor," she asked. "Shall we get a doctor?"

The Professor shook his head. "A doctor wouldn't be able to help me," he said with his eyes tightly closed. They watched him anxiously as the water glass trembled in his hands. Eventually, he opened his eyes and his pupils had regained their normal appearance. "I think I will be fine," he said, "so long as you keep the owl away from me."

Jamie sighed with relief. "Professor, where are the parchments?" he asked.

"They are in my satchel in the other room," replied the Professor.

Jamie put the owl down in the middle of the table and went off to collect the parchments. When he came back he set them before the Professor. Instantly, a faint sheen of sweat appeared on his forehead and his breathing grew sharp. He looked up at Jamie.

"Professor, you are the only one who can read these. You must show me where Fengall is." Jamie said desperately.

The Professor shook his head, his hands clenched tightly. "It would be impossible to find. I cannot say." He slumped back into the chair, his breath now coming in gasps. For many minutes he was silent, just staring at the boy who was looking to him for the answers. He now realised how much he had underestimated the power of that owl. He could see how Murphy had become so fascinated by it. Though he had no idea of its real purpose, he had wanted it for himself. But that small black statue held enough power to have kept a civilisation alive for many centuries and he had been arrogant to think that he could have handled it. He stared back at Jamie. Even if he had his own small magical gift it was hardly a match for the strength of the owl. He could not let the boy go.

Jamie's uneasiness grew with the Professor's continued silence.

"Please, Professor, tell me what's wrong?" he asked finally.

"We might have the owl, but we don't have all the facts; we don't know what is really out there. Without those missing pages, it is far too dangerous even to consider taking the owl back to Fengall."

"But we can't stop now," Jamie cried. "What about the laying of the egg? You said it was vital that the egg be returned to Fengall soon!"

"But not if it costs you your life."

"Professor, if the owl stays here, then we will all be in danger," Jamie replied.

"But the owl has taken the last of my strength and I cannot let you do this alone."

"I won't be alone. Fiona and Fergo will come with me," he said. "And of course, I have the pendant, it will keep us safe."

"Jamie, please listen to me," the Professor implored but Jamie had already made up his mind.

"We'll find a way Professor," he said as he gathered up the parchments and gave them to Fiona. Then picking up the owl they made for the door, leaving the Professor slumped weakly in the chair.

"Come back, Jamie," were the last words they heard as the door closed behind them.

Outside the Professor's shop the rain and wind had eased although the pavements were still awash with rain. As they walked home they got an eerie feeling that they were being watched. Their pace grew slower and slower as they glanced about nervously. Then Fiona made a small startled sound and pointed up towards the roofs of the houses where sitting perched on every window ledge and roof sat row after row of birds. On every pole and chimney stack, birds with their rain-sleeked feathers sat staring as the three passed beneath them. Jamie clutched at the box, the Ebony Owl was safe for the moment.

"C'mon, let's get out of here," he said as they hurried away.

"What happened to the Professor?" Fergo asked as they walked along.

"He shouldn't have looked into the owl's eyes, its power was too strong for him to handle. I have to take it back before it happens to anyone else."

"But what about you?" said Fiona anxiously. "What if the same thing happens to you?"

"The pendant protects me, let's hope it will protect me on the other side of the Gate of Fengall."

That night Jamie did not sleep a wink. He kept thinking about all that had happened. In the end he gave up and just sat in the dark watching the black box which he had left on his dressing table. He could hear a faint clinking sound coming from inside. Eventually he could not resist any longer and he crossed his room and opened the box. Inside, the owl was growing warmer. Jamie could see that it was vibrating ever so slightly, rocking back and forth in the confined space. He quickly shut the lid and jumped back into bed. It was many hours later that Jamie, finally dozing off into an exhausted slumber, was woken by the doorbell.

The sun was shining in through his curtains and he couldn't remember what day it was or even where he was. Then he remembered the owl and the tasks that lay ahead. He jumped up, picked up the owl and called for Fiona but she was already going down the stairs. He heard her open the door and then Fergo's voice. Jamie made for the kitchen where he began laying out the pieces of parchment.

"What are you doing?" Fiona asked as she and Fergo hurried into the kitchen.

Jamie didn't reply. He took the pendant from his pocket and, placing it in his right hand, he held it up to the window and looked through the wee hole in its centre.

"Fiona can you hold the owl for me?" he asked her. She lifted it up, and faced it towards Jamie. Its eyes were glowing dimly as he brought the pendant up so it was aligned with its face. Then the green light intensified as the eyes focused on the pendant. Jamie angled the pendant downwards as the green light blazed down through the hole and over the pages of parchment.

"Fergo move that page this way," he shouted and as Fergo arranged the parchment, they could all see that the beam of green light had changed the unintelligible symbols and lines into a sort of map that they could read.

"Is that the path to the gateway?" Fergo said pointing

to a track that led to the archway in the top corner of the page.

"That must be the way we have to go," Jamie replied.

"It's too dangerous. You can't go through with this," Fiona said firmly, putting the owl down.

"Fiona's right, Jamie. We should wait. Maybe the Professor can still help us," Fergo suggested.

Jamie shook his head. "You saw what happened to Murphy and now to the Professor. The owl's power is immense. If it falls into the wrong hands, who knows what could happen."

The three were so busy arguing that no one noticed the arrival of the big black Range Rover until it screeched to a halt in front of the house. Fergo ran to the door only to see the enraged figure of Murphy striding up the path towards them. He shouted to the others and they all tried to close the door to the porch but they were not quick enough and Murphy reached through grabbing Jamie by the back of his shirt, jolting him backwards and nearly strangling him in the process. Fiona screamed and ran to the phone but Murphy yelled loudly at her.

"Stay where you are, or this'll be the last you'll see of your precious little brother," he growled. Both Fiona and Fergo stopped in their tracks staring at Jamie who was fighting to get away from Murphy.

"Stop struggling," Murphy snarled. "I've only come to ask you some questions."

Fergo gulped as he caught Jamie's eye. He was trying

to be as calm as he could. "What about? We haven't done anything wrong?" he shouted.

Jamie could feel cold sweat trickling down his spine as Murphy gripped him tighter around the shoulders.

"Well my surveillance camera proves you wrong. I got back this morning and watched a very interesting video of four people breaking into my house. Who was the old codger you were with?"

"Nobody, it was nobody," Jamie said flatly.

"So it was nobody who broke my window and helped you replace my owl with some tatty stuffed bird," snapped Murphy angrily. "I *know* you have the owl and I want it back."

Jamie remained defiant. "The owl is not yours. It belongs in Fengall and that is where it is going," he shouted.

Murphy reacted by pushing Jamie roughly away from the open door, away from the prying eyes of any neighbours who might have seen what was going on.

"It's going nowhere. The owl stays with me," he said when he reached the hallway, still with a firm grip on Jamie.

Fergo edged backwards, glancing towards the kitchen table where he knew the owl was sitting in its box.

"I told you what I would do if you so much as set foot near my house," Murphy whispered nastily in Jamie's ear. "Give me my owl back...now."

But Jamie was determined. "The Ebony Owl is not yours and never will be," he said. Despite being half

Murphy's size, he was not going to give in but this only riled Murphy more.

Fiona screamed, "Let him go!" but it made no difference. Then through her tears she turned to Murphy and said coldly, "Let him go, otherwise I'll call the police. We've got photos to prove that there are a lot more strange things in that house of yours than just the owl. I bet the police would like to know where they came from!"

Murphy growled even more deeply and Fiona realised it had been the wrong thing to say. He began to shake Jamie by the collar. But just when it looked like things were about to turn really nasty, they were saved by the postman arriving at the Logan's doorway with a package. Fiona launched herself at Murphy, kicking him in the shins, pummelling his chest and shouting out with all her might. "Help us!" she screamed. "He's going to hurt us!"

Murphy was forced to loosen his grip on Jamie in order to protect himself from the shower of blows. One of Fiona's kicks connected with the bony part of his shin allowing Jamie to escape from his grasp and push him out of the doorway. Murphy had upset the postman's bag causing a flood of envelopes to cascade all over the porch. He skidded on the envelopes and fell, then scrambled to his feet and hobbled away.

Meanwhile, Jamie and Fiona had rushed back to the kitchen. "I'm taking the owl to Fengall now," he whispered to his sister, "before anyone else falls under its power."

"Jamie, you can't! It's too dangerous. You don't know what is out there," Fiona said anxiously. "Please don't go."

"I don't have a choice now. Remember I have Dad's pendant to help me."

Then they heard Fergo shouting, "Run, Jamie, he's coming!" They caught sight of Murphy trying to climb over the side fence and get around to the back of the house. Jamie thrust the parchment map into his pocket as well as the pendant before they sped out of the back door. Murphy had turned back unable to clamber over the fence. He made for the Range Rover.

With the owl secure in the back of Jamie's rucksack the three of them made off on their bikes up the lane that ran along the back of the houses, pedalling as fast as they could. But it was only a second or two before they heard the distinct roar of Murphy's Range Rover sparking into life. They made for the main road not stopping to look back but their hearts sank when the black car appeared behind them.

"He's going to catch us," Jamie shouted and with that they pedalled desperately along the street. They could hear the tyres of Murphy's car screeching as it cornered rapidly trying to keep up with them. Just as Murphy was about to pull alongside, they came to the entrance of the cliff path. Swerving across the road, Jamie, Fergo and Fiona flew up the path forcing Murphy's car to brake violently to avoid hitting the bollards that kept all vehicles out.

When the three eventually stopped to catch their breath they saw the car reverse and drive away.

"He's gone!" Fergo shouted.

"Yes, but not for long. He'll catch up with us by the road," Fiona gasped, breathing heavily.

"Where are we going to go then?" Fergo asked.

Jamie could feel the weight of the owl on his back. "I'm going to try to find Fengall," he said pedalling off.

"But the Professor said you shouldn't go. How are you going to find it?" Fergo called.

Jamie paused, he wasn't too sure himself, but he knew he had to carry on. "We'll find it somehow and I've got the map." He pulled out the pendant from his pocket and placed it into his palm, where immediately the points began to swing. Gradually it stopped with only one point extended slightly as if to show the way north.

He looked at the other two to see that they were staring at him in fright and he knew that his sister was right: it could be far more dangerous than they imagined.

"You don't have to come with me," he said, "but you know the only way to make things right is if I take the owl back." He looked at both of them and turned to set off on his own.

"Wait, Jamie, it's not safe for us here now either. Murphy is after us too," Fiona said as she and Fergo cycled after him. They climbed steadily, only stopping for breath when the path grew too steep. Fergo peered over the edge at the sea where he could see that a small flock of starlings seemed to be following them, gliding on the breeze as they watched their progress up the hill. No one spoke until they were on the top of the cliff and they could hear the surf crashing on the rocks; they began to feel as though they had put some space between themselves and Murphy.

"What path should we...?" Fergo stopped suddenly and pointed ahead. There stood the Fengall warrior in front of them. Above it in the trees, the flock of starlings were now perched and chattering loudly. The warrior took no notice but just stared at them silently from behind its mask.

"Is it going to attack us?" Fiona whispered as the warrior began to take a step towards them but somehow it looked different. Its body was paler and in places it had become transparent. It was as though it was fading away before their eyes. But it was still in their way and the three were not willing to force their way through even if the warrior's power seemed to be dwindling.

Fergo had begun to turn his bike around when in the distance they heard the faint hum of an engine and knew it could be Murphy heading towards them on the coastal road.

"He can't be far behind," Fiona squeaked backing away from the slowly advancing warrior. They knew they couldn't go back down the path but then the warrior stopped. It seemed to take all its strength to raise the heavy lance above its head, pointing it through the glen and on to the high moor.

"Is it showing us the way to go?" Fiona whispered. "Is Fengall that way?"

Jamie consulted the map and placed the pendant upon

it. It too was pointing in that direction. They cycled off, glancing back only once to see if the warrior was still there but it had disappeared. They turned off on to a wide drove road and once they realised they were not being followed by anyone, they felt it was safe enough to slow their pace.

Fergo looked about. Everything was quiet and normal. "Are you sure we are going the right way?" he asked at last.

"Well, at least it's somewhere Murphy won't think of looking for us," Fiona said. But when they stopped for a rest, they thought they could still hear the faint hum of an engine.

"That Range Rover is a four wheel drive," groaned Fergo. "Murphy will have no problems following us."

But Jamie had other problems to think about. He had begun to feel the heat radiating from the owl in his rucksack. He stopped and took the rucksack off his back. He stretched his shoulders and glanced in at the owl which was now rocking quite steadily within its case. The other two stopped behind and stared hard at him. He managed a wan smile, but uneasily he noticed the birds that had come to perch in the gorse around them, cheeping and chirping. Then over the horizon, the sun glinted on something bright. Jamie's heart sank: it was the reflection from a windscreen and they all knew it was Murphy's car heading over the moorland towards them.

"He'll spot us soon," Fergo screeched, but there was nowhere for them to hide, as there were hardly any trees.

"Head for the glen, we might get some cover in there," Jamie suggested and with that they cycled on followed by their band of feathered companions.

The trees in the glen gave them some cover but the sound of Murphy's car never seemed that far away. They continued on, knowing that he was out there somewhere, searching for them. The first seeds of panic began to grow in Jamie's mind. He wondered what would happen to them if they did not discover the mysterious Gate of Fengall, but also, what was to become of them if they did!

It was just after midday and they were cycling across open country again in order to follow the direction shown by the pendant. They had not heard any engines for some time now and luckily this part of the moor was quite dry so it was not difficult for them to cycle quite fast among the heather, following the well worn paths made by flocks of sheep.

"Where do you think the gateway is?" Fiona asked.

"I can't go on much further," panted Fergo.

Though there was still a few hours of daylight left, the sun was beginning to disappear into a thick bank of cloud and a mist started to roll in from the west. By chance, they found themselves skirting around a small loch. They could hear the faint lap of the waves beside them but it was Fergo who blundered into the water without realising where he was going. He got off his bike and sprinkled water on his face.

"If this is the loch then we're at least ten miles from

home," he stated. "No wonder we're so tired."

"The Gate of Fengall has to be here somewhere," Jamie said, as suddenly the points of the pendant began to swing erratically. The mist was now obscuring everything and the owl was becoming heavier and heavier on his back. Just as he was wondering how they could go on any further, the pendant's movements became so strange that Jamie began to feel dizzy. He lost all sense of direction and Fiona and Fergo's voices disappeared over the sound of shouting and yelling. He had been transported back to the battle with Fengall. He could see their bright red banners flying in front of him. He could see the soldiers ahead fighting valiantly but then came a sound from behind the ranks, from right where Jamie was standing. Around him the great sorcerers had begun to chant out their spells and incantations. Now Jamie heard himself joining in. He knew each and every word by heart and he spoke with great confidence as he too began to advance across the field.

Then it seemed no more than a second later when he heard Fiona screaming out his name. He came around to see his sister staring down at him lying on the ground.

"Jamie, get up. You've got to see this." She was staring at the ground all around him which was covered in old spears, pieces of armour, swords and broken banners. They were scattered on the grass as far as the eye could see. Misty tendrils swept in between them making them look ghostly. Fiona and Fergo were scared, but Jamie had seen it all before and he realised that he knew what to do. He opened his palm and the pendant gleamed. He held it high above his head as the points began to spin faster and faster in Jamie's hand. Fergo and Fiona stood back to watch as Jamie, holding the pendant above his head walked forward. Then Fiona screamed as she saw the pendant flash. A bolt of white lightning struck from sky to earth. Jamie did not flinch, but continued on across the littered field. A second later, all three of them heard a loud cracking noise and then just ahead of them, out of the mist, a great dark archway loomed. The mist swirled for a moment and then settled, like a draught had been blown through a suddenly opened door.

"There it is – there's the gate," Fergo shouted and indeed before them, they could all see a solitary stone archway just like the picture on the parchment.

"It's not what I imagined," said Fiona as she stared at the arch. There was no fence or wall on either side, but simply a stile in the middle of it. "It's not a very good gate...it doesn't keep anything in," Fiona remarked.

They left their bicycles on the battlefield, a little way from the arch and went over for a closer look.

"It certainly looks old," Fiona said as they got nearer. It looked as though it had stood undisturbed and unnoticed in the middle of the moor for hundreds of years. Dark green ivy and moss wound its way up and around the arch. When Jamie looked closely at the ancient structure he wondered if it was just the ivy that was holding the whole thing together. The stone had begun to crumble and bits lay strewn all over the ground.

Fiona reached out a hand and touched it. The mist that now surrounded them was thick and made the moss and ivy wet to the touch. She recoiled her hand from the slimy surface and brushed it down her jacket. "Ugh, it feels disgusting."

Fergo was standing staring through the arch as Fiona walked around to the right of it. She thought this would transport her into the land of Fengall, and she waited to feel a change, but nothing happened and the swirling mist and the sound of distant bleating sheep was just the same.

Fergo walked around to the left of the arch and they made faces at each other from either side. The archway looked just as old and as mouldy as it had from the front.

They just walked back around in time to hear Jamie's voice disappear into thin air, "Come and look at th..."

All they could see were Jamie's wet footprints in the mud around the wooden stile. They ran back around to the sides to see if there was any sign of him, but all they could see was the moor stretching out for miles before them. Fiona was the first to follow him through. She simply disappeared in front of Fergo's eyes.

"Hey, come back, you're not leaving me on my own," shouted Fergo in a frightened voice. He looked back at the pile of bikes and thought how normal they looked compared to what could be lying beyond that crumbling gate. But what gave him the biggest chill of fear was being left behind to face Murphy on his own. Summoning up his courage, he took a deep breath and rushed through the gateway. He nearly fell over the others who were standing on the other side just watching the skyline for any sound or movement, for there was no wind, no sound – nothing but a deathly silence. The archway looked exactly as it had on the other side except it seemed to have crumbled more and the grass was strewn with small bits of rubble. As they stood there, several small fragments of rubble fell from the arch on to the ground.

"It's not going to stand up for much longer," said Fergo.

"Maybe it's because the people of Fengall don't have much time left," said Jamie as he checked the points of the pendant.

Fiona was sniffing the air. She thought it seemed thinner as though there was less oxygen in the air on this side of the gate.

Meanwhile, Jamie had glanced back and noticed that their bikes were still visible on the other side of the archway. But then they heard a sound like thunder, but it did not die out, instead it just grew louder and louder. They stood in silence and soon the source of the noise was upon them. They only realised what it was when they saw that the dark cloud was filled with wings as a great flock of birds flew towards the Fengall gate. The noise became deafening as bird after bird flew through the gateway and then disappeared, into the mist. The three had to cover their heads with their hands as the flapping wings passed only a hair's breadth above them. In less than two minutes most of the birds had passed and only a few stragglers were left.

They stood up and surveyed the scene. "Now that you've opened the gateway Jamie, it looks like those birds are returning home to Fengall," Fiona commented. They all glanced back to see their bikes which seemed a reassuring sign. Jamie hitched up his rucksack, the owl weighing heavily as he turned back towards Fengall. But then Fiona grabbed his arm, her eyes wide with alarm. She pointed back through the gate. Jamie turned about and there in the distance they could see headlights making straight for them through the mist.

"He's found us. Murphy must have seen our tracks," Fergo cried out. "C'mon, we have to go on."

They ran as fast as they could following the flock of birds which had now become a dark speck in the sky.

At first, the land seemed familiar, patches of thistles were scattered about, but there were no sheep and no longer any bird noise. Everything seemed suspended silently in time. The sun had now disappeared completely into the thickening mist and it was difficult to judge whether night was closing in or another day was about to begin.

As they wandered on Fiona and Fergo pulled their jackets tightly around them as the temperature slowly began to drop. Jamie did not feel the cold as the owl on his back was giving out warmth. It radiated through the rucksack like a hot water bottle.

They trudged on a bit further until Fiona's teeth began to chatter.

"Here, you take the owl. It's like a radiator...it will

warm you up," Jamie told his sister and gratefully she took the rucksack.

"It's the first time the owl has come in handy," Fiona remarked as she hoisted it on to her back.

"Don't worry about me," Fergo said. "I've got my coat and look, I've just found this in my pocket…Anyone want some?" Fergo said pulling a rather squashed bar of chocolate from his pocket. He didn't notice the wrapper fall from the hole in his pocket as he took a large bite out of the chocolate bar as they stumbled onwards.

Soon the path became littered with stones. At first it was small pebbles in the grass but soon their ankles were being turned on hidden stones and finally rocky outcrops made walking in a straight line impossible. They had to use the pendant constantly to keep them heading in the right direction through the mist.

The smallest of breezes had picked up which made the late afternoon even cooler and soon the ground underfoot became damp and the rocks slippery as they climbed over them. Eventually they were forced to stop and rest. Fergo took the rucksack for a while as Fiona had grown tired with the weight but there was nowhere to sit down as moss now clung to the rocks and water dripped from rivulets on to the ground.

"This place is weird. It is as though we are climbing up into a cloud or up a mountain without a slope."

A drizzly rain began to fall and Fiona put her hood up as they trudged on, keeping as close together as they could.

"We've been walking for miles," said Fiona eventually when they stopped by a small group of young rowan saplings standing by a gurgling stream.

"At least a hundred miles by the way my feet hurt," said Fergo.

"I wonder what we are going to find when we get there," said Fiona. "We could be out here all night."

"But we've come this far, we can't turn back now," Jamie said firmly.

"And I can feel that the owl has got warmer...I hope it doesn't lay the egg here," said Fergo handing the owl back to Jamie.

"Let's take a look at it; a wee peek won't hurt."

They all huddled round as Jamie removed the owl from his rucksack. He slowly pulled back the top to reveal what he thought was a piece of smouldering coal. The Ebony Owl's shiny eyes gleamed out at him; its body had become shiny and smooth with the heat. But, it was not yet hot enough to burn them and so they were able to return some of the feeling to their cold and numb fingers by holding their hands over the owl's body. Fiona and Fergo were careful not to look too keenly at the owl's eyes but they could both see that nearly all the white feathers had gone, the last of them lay charred in the bottom of the parcel and as Fiona looked closely at the solid black body she saw some strange markings on its small round stomach. Though the other two avoided staring directly at it, as long as Jamie held the pendant in front of him, he had no problems looking into the owl's eyes.

"It won't be long before the owl lays the egg."

"How do you know that?" Fiona asked him.

"Because of the pictures in the Professor's papers. When it laid the egg, it grew very hot. I don't think it is ready yet."

They hastily packed the owl back into the bag and set off into the steady downpour of rain. Around them the landscape had changed yet again. Instead of just boulders and rocks there were small shrubs and young trees sprouting from the rocks around them. Soon they were walking through knee high fern and bracken and they had to be careful to avoid the hidden rocks and vines underneath. With their heads down they did not notice the trees were getting taller.

As they continued the trees grew older and more knarled around them, as though they had entered an ancient forest. The rain had eased to a drizzle but when they pulled their hats off and looked behind them, they could see the rain was still falling heavily on the moor.

"The rain hasn't stopped at all, it's just that it can't get through the canopy of leaves above us," said Fiona looking skywards.

Fergo found another squashed bar of chocolate. Jamie and Fiona were so hungry that they didn't care about the fluff; they took a big bite each. Then, as they wandered towards a rise, the first in an otherwise flat landscape, they noticed how the stones had become icy and stepping up through a rocky escarpment they found pockets of snow hidden in furrows on the ground.

"It hasn't been cold enough to snow for ages," said Fergo.

"Yes, but we are not in our own Scotland any more, this is Fengall. The weather is obviously very different here," said Jamie jumping over an icy puddle.

Soon they were negotiating their way through deeper drifts while the trees around them grew more and more dense. It was not long before the overhanging branches were scratching their faces at every step. In some places the trees had grown so close together that they had to walk sideways in order to squeeze through the gaps.

After a while they had to stop and rest as they were all exhausted. They hunkered down beside a rock even though the ground was cold and wet. No one had the energy to speak until some minutes later Fergo sat bolt upright. He glanced at the others but they had dozed off. Fergo stared out into the mist. There was nothing to see except the dense greyness but then he heard a faint mumble of voices. Someone was running fast, and with every step they were getting closer to them but though Fergo strained his eyes peering into the fog, he could not see a thing.

Finally, the voices grew loud enough for him to hear what was being said. "'Ere Guv, let's go home. I can't see a thing and the footprints have gone again," one man called.

"Just keep trying, they must be around here somewhere and my owl's with 'em," came the gruff reply.

The sound of that voice chilled Fergo to the bone. He

looked down and now he could see that in the soft ground they had been leaving a trail of well defined prints.

"It's Murphy, he's found us," he whispered shaking the others awake. In an instant, they were on their feet and for a panicked second all three of them ran in different directions. Fiona took off blindly, her heart hammering in panic until she struck what she thought was a tree but then a pair of arms began to encircle her. She screamed and tore herself free diving off into the mist again while calling out to Jamie and Fergo. They found each other by sheer chance and stood, listening to Murphy shouting at his men to run after them. They ran on, turning back every few steps to see if they were being followed, but no one appeared through the mist.

They only slowed up when the sound of Murphy's voice was far in the distance. Then after a few minutes rest, they gathered up the last of their strength and forced themselves onwards, as best they could.

"Are you sure this is the right way," Fergo whispered some moments later, tearing his coat which was snagged between the trunks of two trees.

But Jamie was certain. "The pendant's still pointing this way," he said.

After another half an hour, Jamie had to stop to remove the rucksack from his back to negotiate his way through the trees. It was then that he noticed the first sound of a bird they had heard in a long while. It sounded like the gentle cooing of a dove. For so many miles there had been absolute silence but now they could hear a faint cheep and then they saw a flutter of wings in the branches above them.

"Did you see that?" said Jamie looking up into the trees.

They stopped and looked around them, and there, far above in the high tree tops, several birds were perched, chattering frantically.

"They're watching us," whispered Fiona.

"I can feel it too. And I think wherever we are going these birds know we're on our way," said Jamie as he watched one bird fly away in the direction they were about to take.

Within another two or three more paces their steps were slowed by the sudden appearance of giant rocks covered in a mantle of snow which they had to climb over. It was at that point that they realised that the noise from the birds had increased and when Jamie looked up he could see that there were so many birds, the tree branches were bending with the weight. There were birds of every variety chirping away and fluttering between branches. Some varieties Jamie had never seen before. The three of them kept on, walking as close together as they could for safety.

Then Fergo yelled out as one bird dived down at him. Fiona clutched at Jamie's coat and glanced fearfully up into the branches. She saw a dozen black and white magpies suddenly fly up from the branches and head off, then many others took off in a loud flurry of wings.

"What happened? Did something frighten them?" Fiona asked.

They all stopped in their tracks and at that moment they heard a faint rumble from deep under their feet. The whole forest floor began to shake from the earthquake and the snow in the trees fell to the ground in mini avalanches all around them. Suddenly, without warning, the snowy floor beneath them began to crack and then a great hole opened up swallowing rocks and small plants into its depths.

They tried to grab hold of loose tree branches as they were plummeted down through the drift. Snow went into their mouths and noses as they were jettisoned down a long shoot towards a dark and unknown place below.

12
Capture

When they landed, on what seemed to be a bed of soft cushioned heather, they were all blinded by the snow in their eyes. Fergo, who had grabbed on to the branch of a tree to stop himself falling was still holding on to it when he landed. He was covered in leaves and mud, while Fiona's hair was covered with snow and her hair had stuck to her face, obscuring her view completely. She sat spitting out snow and hair while trying to make out what it was they had landed on in the dark tunnel.

Jamie, blinking his way through the mud, was the first to realise that they were in some sort of green glade, as there was no snow on the ground. It felt much warmer. His breath was no longer visible in the air as it had been above ground. As their eyes adjusted to the dim light they could tell that the glade led into a tree-lined tunnel, the leafy branches forming a natural ceiling, while at the end of that they could just make out a lighted cavern.

"Is everyone okay?" Jamie asked, scrambling quickly to his feet.

"I think so," said Fergo, getting rid of an insect from his ear with a shake of his head.

They stood up and shaking themselves down, they ventured a few steps towards the light. At first in the dimness it seemed that the trees were growing closely together but then Fiona screamed as one of the trees began to move.

When she looked closely she saw that behind each tree was a group of tall masked birdmen each with a long metal spear in its hand. Fergo yelled out for they were nearly as tall and as broad as the trees themselves but dressed in cloaks made of woven leaves which made them hard to see against the natural backdrop of trees. Fiona cowered away as a line of these masked birdmen warriors began to edge towards them, the green light of their eyes filtering through from behind their masks.

It was then that Jamie noticed that birds were sitting on each of their shoulders. The warriors in front were adorned with ospreys and kestrels, while at the back on the shoulders of the taller warriors, crouched sparrow hawks, falcons, and eagles all staring at them with their round unblinking eyes. Jamie had never seen anything like it before.

Then all at once, the birds began to make a noise. Fergo thought it was like walking past the cages of birds at the zoo, but as the warriors started to close in around them, he decided he was the one who felt like the caged animal. None of the warriors came close enough to touch them, but instead, using their spears, they slowly nudged them along the tunnel towards the lighted cavern at the end.

Soon more and more of these birds began to cheep and caw and whistle as they passed underneath. "If what the Professor said was true," Jamie whispered, "then all these birds must have once been warriors themselves."

"It's all too strange," whispered Fiona. "I want to wake up in my own bed and find out this is all a horrible dream."

They walked forwards clutching each other as more and more of the birdmen with sharp lances formed a line behind them. The bird song was loud within the cavern and the chirping and fluttering of wings echoed loudly in the air. They soon found themselves at the entrance to the chamber and they stopped, not willing to go out into the brightly lit cavern, but prodded forwards by the tips of the lances, and they had no choice but to move.

They stumbled into the light and found themselves in an underground cavern the size of a football pitch. There were great majestic wooden pillars holding up the ceiling, but instead of elegant chandeliers and furnishings, the only decorations were wooden lanterns suspended from the foliage covered roof. Natural light fed in from holes on the two long sides and the three could see that it was the roots from the trees above ground which had formed a natural mosaic pattern on the ceiling. They tried to stop to take all this in but were pushed forward as the numbers of warriors swelled behind them, forcing them out into the middle of the chamber like a cork from a bottle. They stumbled forward until they were in front of a large platform raised by two lighted trees acting as pillars on either side.

Jamie could feel the intense heat of the owl now coming through his jacket and he was forced to carry the rucksack in his outstretched arms. He could feel that since the bird calls had begun in the chamber, the Ebony Owl had started to rock quite violently within the rucksack.

Just as Fiona was about to put her hands over her ears to lessen the din, the noise ceased altogether and a figure in a full-length feather cloak appeared above them out of a walkway at the very top of the cavern. It stood motionless, looking down at them with its head inclined to the side, blinking its light green eyes like an owl stalking mice in a dimly lit barn. But then it began to speak in a deep gravelly voice that sounded more human than birdlike. Jamie froze. He recognised the voice as the one that had called to him from the garden. The voice that had told him to find the owl.

"Welcome to Fengall, Jamie," the great creature said, bending towards them, a small smile creasing the corners of its birdlike mouth. "Your arrival brings us much happiness." Then the smile turned into a deep throaty laugh which echoed and vibrated throughout the whole chamber. The three stood in stunned silence as they looked at the creature with its long brown tresses of hair the colour of dark nourished earth, and a beard as dense and as thick as a bush in full leaf.

Jamie was frightened as they were trapped by the army of now silent warriors at their backs and the approach of this menacing figure from the front. He held out his pendant defiantly and it flashed in the light.

"Your new found magic will not help you here," the towering creature declared as it stared down at Jamie intently, "but it has served you well on your journey." Then the birdlike creature laughed its evil laugh again.

Jamie realised in that second that they had walked into a trap! The Professor had been right; they should have waited. He clutched the pendant tightly but it would not respond to him. How was he going to get Fergo and Fiona out of there safely? Was it up to him to try and destroy Fengall? Had his dreams been leading him to this? But before he had a chance to think further his captors, at the creature's insistence, dragged Fergo and Fiona away from him and bound their hands together, attaching them to the walls with thick ropes.

Now there was nothing they could do but watch as the birdmen began to rejoice with laughter and songs which echoed around the cavern and it was several minutes before the creature silenced them with a harsh vulture-like screech. Jamie's face was bright red and it was not just from the warmth of the owl, he knew that he had been outwitted. Finally the cavern fell silent as the birdmen took their positions at the head of the chamber.

Fergo, his hands aching from the binding on his wrists, struggled for a moment but it was useless.

"Jamie, why are they holding us like this?" he shouted. "We brought the owl back here. Why aren't they grateful?"

The great birdlike creature turned and strode over growing more menacing with every stride.

"Gratitude is something that I, Hawkshead, leader of these Fengall people can never give to you, not when you are returning what is rightfully ours. Your people caused our destruction. Now it is you who will pay."

Jamie suddenly felt very cold and sick. How could he have let Fiona and Fergo be dragged into this?

Hawkshead looked out at the ranks of his leaf clad warriors that filled the hall. Then he raised his arms and the birds rose from the warriors' shoulders and flew up to perch on any branch or twig they could find in the walls and ceiling of the cavern.

A great murmur went around the hall as Hawkshead inclined his great head towards his birdmen as though he was signifying the victory of a great battle. He then closed his arms around himself and took a bow. "Our waiting is over my brothers. The Ebony Owl has been returned." The roar from the crowd was deafening.

When the din had stopped Hawkshead continued. "Soon our lives will be restored and we will be strong and powerful once again." Behind him a great cry of triumph echoed through the cavern. Hawkshead silenced every creature with a single swish of his cloak.

"Now give me the Ebony Owl," he said, turning back to Jamie. "Too much time has been wasted. Our lost idol must be returned to its rightful place before we lose our lives forever."

Jamie tried to cling tightly to the rucksack but the heat from the owl was beginning to burn through the canvas material and singe his jacket. He stared up at Hawkshead whose claw-like hand was beckoning towards him. There was nothing he could do but take the Ebony Owl from his bag.

A white hot hiss of steam rose into the air as the owl was revealed. Hawkshead yelled triumphantly and clapped his hands when he saw it.

"The time has come. We must prepare for the arrival of the crystal egg," Hawkshead shouted, and many of the birdmen left the chamber while the birds flew about the branches of the ceiling. Then Hawkshead turned to the three children.

"What you see before you is all that is left of a once great race. For every birdman warrior that stands before you, a thousand more have fallen because our owl was taken from us."

His head, with its thick feathered neck, slowly rotated in a far greater arc than any human spine would have permitted as he glanced behind him to the ranks of waiting birdmen. He turned back and strode over until he was so close to the three of them that they were choked by the smell of forest and damp leaves emanating from his cloak. He was so tall that they barely reached above his waist. He had to bend his body in half to look them in the eyes.

Jamie pulled back as far as he could against the wall.

Fergo was astounded by the creature's green saucer-sized eyes as they blinked slowly like a bird watching its prey.

"Give me the owl, Jamie, or you will never see your friends again," he stated firmly.

At that moment a great roar filled the cavern as a group of the Fengall warriors returned carrying a black cylindrical-shaped podium which they fitted into a shaft in the floor in the middle of the cavern. Jamie could see that the middle of the podium was hollow and that once the owl laid the egg, it would travel down the shaft and into a chasm far below. Then the Fengalls would have their power back. Somehow he had to stop that happening. He watched as the podium was finally fixed in place and a roar went up. Birds flew up into the air chirping wildly, their wings hitting one another causing feathers to float to the ground like the contents of a torn cushion.

When the roar had died down, Hawkshead said, "The ceremony is about to begin." He motioned to Jamie but Jamie knew he couldn't give the owl up. It was their only hope. He put it behind his back and flattened himself against the wall.

"Let them go first," Jamie cried out.

Hawkshead's only response was to laugh even louder. "I cannot do that for as soon as the crystal egg has restored our strength, we intend to invade your human world now that the gateway has been reopened between our two worlds." Hawkshead's eyes glittered with a deep hatred.

"This time however, we will be the victors."

Through the ropes, Fiona linked Fergo's hand into hers as Jamie moved over to stand in front of them, the Ebony Owl clutched tightly in his hands.

Hawkshead bowed down towards them. "One mortal life will be taken for every Fengall warrior who has lost his." He strode away from them across the cavern but then turned quickly pointing his long arm in their direction. "Starting with yours, if you do not co-operate. Now give me the owl!" he screeched.

All three of them jumped in fright and Fergo screamed which only made Hawkshead laugh.

"You can't do this. Let us go!" Fiona shouted out. "We don't know anything.

Hawkshead looked puzzled at this remark. "Oh, but you do. You now know the plans I have in store for the human world!" he said, shaking his head.

Then he laughed again and without another word wrenched the Ebony Owl away from Jamie. He placed it on top of the podium where everyone in the cavern could see it pulsating strongly, as though it now had a heartbeat of its own. Its green eyes were now tinged with a dull red in their very centre. The owl was getting hotter. Jamie knew they had only minutes before the egg would be laid. Then he remembered the Professor who not only knew about Fengall but knew that they had gone to find it. Maybe there was a chance.

"You won't get far," Jamie shouted defiantly. "There are others who know where we are. Already, they are organising an army who'll be ready and waiting for you when you reach the gate."

All Hawkshead did was laugh. "You cannot threaten me, boy," he screeched.

"Jamie, you're making it worse," said Fiona shutting her eyes tightly as she tried to break free from the ropes.

Several of the birdmen had moved closer to Jamie, pointing their spears at his head forcing him to watch the owl.

"It is time for the Fengalls to rise again! The crystal is ready to be laid," said Hawkshead as he stared at the shuddering owl.

At that moment there was a flurry of wings and a few anguished cries from the mouth of the cavern. Fergo and Fiona struggled to try and free themselves, but the ropes did not slacken an inch. Then they heard the loud crack of a pistol and a feeble cry. They stopped struggling.

"Jamie, what was that?" Fiona yelled, as she saw one of Hawkshead's warriors slump to the ground. But by the time it had fallen only a pile of robes lay scattered on the ground while out of the sleeve fluttered a small feathery bird.

Then they heard a voice they all recognised.

"What is going on here?" It was without a doubt the voice of Murphy. They saw him standing in doorway, his mouth wide open in astonishment. Behind him, his two men gaped openly at the scene before them but their weapons were cocked ready as they slowly stepped into the chamber. Warily, they advanced across the floor until

Murphy and his henchmen were walking through the crowd of leaf clad birdmen towards the front. Murphy's men looked about them in disbelief, with terror in their eyes while Murphy, caring only about finding the owl, strode boldly forward.

They were not as tall as the birdmen warriors who surrounded them, but they looked as strong. Hawkshead's warriors looked to him for a command, they were unwilling to tackle these men with their powerful weapons.

"Is this your conquering army, Jamie?" he laughed as he became aware of Murphy forcing his way through the crowd towards him. "Attack him, he is only mortal," he commanded his men.

The warriors rallied to his call but one of their number fell to the floor, the victim of one of Murphy's bullets and once again, the warrior transformed, this time into a magpie. The Fengall warriors drew back. It was not the time to engage in fighting when their powers were at their lowest ebb. Without the power of the Ebony Owl's egg, they could not risk another of their dwindling numbers.

By now Murphy had reached the platform and the three children could see him clearly. His eyes were crazed with greed and madness and he did not seem to realise how threatening Hawkshead was as he towered above him. Fergo shivered violently. Something bad was about to happen.

"The owl is mine. I was the one who found it," Fergo

heard Murphy say. An odd mesmerised smile appeared on his face as he stared in rapture at the Ebony Owl. His fingers carefully reached out towards the gleaming green eyes. Only then did he notice Jamie and the others cowering in the corner and shouted at them. "This is all your fault. You had no right taking my owl away from me."

"The Ebony Owl is not yours and never will be," came Hawkshead's reply. His voice was so loud it reverberated off the walls of the cavern. "You may have felt the great magic within the owl but its power belongs here, not in human hands." Hawkshead then pulled himself up to his full height.

"You don't frighten me!" Murphy retorted, the strong urge to have the owl to himself overcoming all fears. But then Hawkshead moved in and Murphy suddenly realised how big he really was. Through his crazed senses, he at last sensed that Hawkshead may hold the advantage. He changed his tactics and took a step backwards, his eyes narrowing and a small smirk forming on his lips. He still wanted the owl at any cost.

"Maybe we could make a deal," he said, rubbing his hands together. "I have many jewels and lavish treasures which I would be willing to exchange for just the owl."

Hawkshead roared with laughter bearing down on Murphy regardless of the two guns that were levelled at him. Murphy began to circle him, all the time getting closer to the children. Soon he was standing right beside Jamie and the others.

"How did you get here?" Jamie asked him, his small voice echoing out from within the tree-like embrace of his captor. Murphy glanced towards him, but his aim on Hawkshead's chest did not waiver.

"It was easy, all I had to do was just follow your tracks," he said laughing at them. "They led me right here to you and your peculiar friends..." Then he swung his full attention back to Hawkshead and the gun jerked menacingly with his every word. "...And to the owl," he said as he began to climb towards the pillar that held the glowing, pulsating Ebony Owl. Hawkshead grabbed his coat, nearly lifting him off the ground but Murphy was not to be put off. He turned and swung his gun at Hawkshead, glancing a blow at his chest which caused a fight to begin that flung clumps of feathers into the air. Hawkshead's warriors came to their leader's rescue and for a moment they were distracted from Jamie and the others by the fight going on around them.

Jamie twisted and squirmed to get free from his captor. Without being seen, he took the pendant from his pocket. He felt a charge from it and rubbed it between his fingers until the points extended in his palm. Hawkshead was wrong, even in the Fengall stronghold, some of its power was still there. He edged over towards the others and used the sharp points to hack at the ropes until finally the fibres tore, releasing Fiona. She rubbed her wrists and helped him loosen the ropes that held Fergo.

"Run for it," Jamie cried and with that the three ran for their lives, only to be cut off by a group of warriors who were heading straight for them.

"This way," said Jamie, heading back towards the pillar with the Ebony Owl. They were now right in the very midst of the fight. Murphy's men had finally been overcome. Three warriors were holding each man's arms but then Murphy, in a last attempt, dived on to a group of birdmen in front of them. Fergo was catapulted out of the way. For a second he flew through the air heading straight towards the podium. He hit it with a loud thud and then looked up to see the Ebony Owl rocking on top of its pedestal.

"Jamie!" he shouted as at the moment the Ebony Owl dropped like a stone towards the hard ground of the cavern.

Jamie saw the owl topple over and ran as fast as he could towards it. He managed to catch it with one hand but had to let it go instantly as it was too hot to hold. However, he had broken its fall and the Ebony Owl rolled intact across the floor, charring the leaves that lay beneath it. Jamie picked it up as best he could and put it inside his bag.

Neither Hawkshead nor Murphy had seen the owl dislodged. Nor did they see the three small figures run for all they were worth over the top, around and under the fighting bodies.

As they reached the mouth of the cavern, their hearts leapt into their mouths as they heard another round of gunfire ring out and then silence. Both Hawkshead and Murphy turned to see the three of them escaping. They had no chance now. But then Jamie had an idea. He felt for the pendant and squeezing it tightly, he felt it grow warm in his palm. He took it from his pocket and threw it down on to the floor where it bounced once and then exploded in a fit of sparks and fire. The cavern became filled with a dense blue smoke.

They did not wait around to see what happened. Jamie caught the pendant as it whirled back and they ran as fast as they could. The noise of the birds around them was deafening but it was not as loud as the enraged yell they heard from Hawkshead and his men. It sent them running up the darkened tunnel, feeling their way as they went.

"Look out!" shouted Fergo, "They're going to attack." At that moment an evil-looking black and white magpie dived at him. They all hid their heads in their coats to try to avoid the beaks and claws of the birds that were waiting in the trees to attack them. The birds began to screech loudly.

"It's warning the others," Jamie shouted, as he forced his way onwards through the flurry of wings towards the light at the top of the tunnel.

He helped Fiona climb up but the soles of her shoes were slippery and each time she tried to find a foothold, she slipped further back. Finally, the ground gave way underneath her causing more earth to fill in the entrance to the tunnel. With Fergo and Jamie pulling her arms, she managed to clamber up. They looked back at the hole and saw that the tunnel would have to be cleared. They had gained a few moments.

"They'll soon catch us up," Fergo said as they ploughed on through the snowdrifts.

Although they were exhausted they ran as though their lives depended on it, forcing their way over dead trees and over the icy ground. They soon became oblivious to the branches that scratched their faces and ripped at their clothes. The birds in the forest tried to stop them leaving. Jamie felt in his pocket for the now cool pendant. He hurled it at the birds who swooped in too close. It struck a jackdaw and then, like a boomerang, it returned to him. Soon their feathered attackers withdrew and kept their distance from the small human and his sharp and painful missile.

They only began to slow their pace when the land beneath their feet became heathery and the trees of the strange forest began to thin, letting in the reflection of the moonlight.

"Which way do we go now?" asked Fergo looking out at the moor which looked the same in every direction. Even the pendant did not seem able to help them.

"What are we going to do?" Fiona asked. She was close to tears. She slumped down and put her head into her grimy hands and pressed her fingers to her eyes. They all knew that Hawkshead and possibly Murphy could be close behind them. But then Fergo pointed and ran forward.

"Look! There's the wrapper from my chocolate bar!" he yelled, and then he spotted their footprints. "Come on, it must be this way." And with that they were off running again.

Even though their breaths were burning their lungs and every muscle in their legs ached, they tried to keep up the pace, passing over the rain-soaked rocky ground until eventually, just as their strength began to fail, they came in sight of the Gate of Fengall.

"There's the archway!" gasped Fiona.

They allowed their pace to slow but at that moment the Ebony Owl had become so hot it burned out through the bottom of Jamie's bag. It hit the rocky ground with a loud thud and smashed. Fiona screamed and Jamie fell to his knees, searching the ground. With their breath coming in ragged gulps they stared blankly at the remains of the powerful Ebony Owl.

Fergo attempted to pick up the pieces. "Where are its eyes?" he shouted. They all bent to search but pieces of the owl were now scattered all around. Jamie picked up small pieces of the owl that lay strewn among rocks and pebbles and grass, but the eyes were gone. No one could find them.

Then close behind them they heard an eerie screech.

"We can't waste any more time," said Fiona. "They must be gaining on us by now."

Dragging Fergo, Fiona began to run ahead but at that moment Jamie spied something glinting in the grass. He bent down and saw lying in the midst of the shattered pieces of black owl, a milk-white stone the size of a fist. Without stopping, Jamie bent and picked it up and put it straight into a pocket of his charred rucksack.

Fergo and Fiona were the first to reach the gate. It was now a lot smaller and seemed less daunting. Fiona was the first to run through, just in time to avoid a large rock from the top of the arch from hitting her. It crumbled on the ground followed by another avalanche of smaller rocks and rubble. Jamie and Fergo did not wait around to see if the arch was going to give way altogether and bundled through after her.

Back in their own world, the air seemed sweeter and the wind carried the smell of the sea so many miles away. But their relief was short lived when Fiona pointed to the place where they had left their bikes – Murphy had driven his Range Rover right over the top of them. All they could see was the mangled remains of buckled wheels and frames poking out under the back tyres.

"Och no, I don't believe it," shouted Fiona nearly in tears. "What are we going to do now?"

"It's too late to do anything," Fergo announced. "Can you hear that?"

For a moment they were all silent. They were looking at the archway and although there was nothing to see from the Fengall side, the sound of screeching birds and the thunderous roar of pounding feet were growing louder with every second. Then they saw the flock of speeding scout birds sent on ahead to find them. A moment later, just inside the gate, they could make out the thundering crowd of warlike birdmen armed with spears.

"We're going to die!" wailed Fergo.

The sight of these pale ghostlike warriors put fear into the hearts of all of three of them. There was nowhere for them to hide.

"Get behind the car, it's our only hope," cried Fergo. Across the open ground they fled, never looking back until they were hidden by the black Range Rover.

"Please let it be open," said Fiona as she pulled at every door. Miraculously, the driver's door sprung open. "Get in!" she cried. Fergo and Jamie piled in behind her locking all the doors.

Nearly frightened out of their wits, they stared out through the windscreen of the car at the approaching flock of birds and birdmen. It looked like a swarm of black bees devouring the landscape in its wake.

"They're closing in on us! What are we going to do?" said Fiona panicking wildly.

The scout birds were already through the arch and within a few seconds they had reached the car. They landed on the roof and began to scratch it with their talons, as though trying to tear through the metal. Inside, the sound was unbearable – it was like fingernails scraping down a blackboard.

Fiona burst into tears. "They are going to kill us!" she screamed.

By now the group of warriors had passed through the Gate of Fengall and into the real world.

Jamie sitting in the back seat felt a cold grip of fear tearing at his stomach when he recognised the tall figure of Hawkshead in the midst of the angry mob. He seemed to stride just above the ground, half walking, half flying. The rest of the warriors were brandishing spears and swords.

Soon the whole car was surrounded. The three scrambled around the seats staring out of the windows at the warriors. In the scramble Fergo's foot fell down between the two front seats. Without realising it, he let off the handbrake and slowly, the car began to move forward down the slight incline. The Fengall warriors scattered as the car rolled faster.

Fergo looked up and screamed as he saw Hawkshead now at the front of the bunch, striding angrily towards the car.

They all yelled as a warrior hurled his spear at the bonnet but instead of striking the car, it simply turned into a long black feather. Another spear struck the windscreen but again, the same thing happened. Without the egg from the Ebony Owl, the Fengall power had not been restored. But this did not stop Hawkshead who came on relentlessly.

Suddenly the car, which was now rolling steadily, hit a rut, turning the wheels; it began to head towards Hawkshead. Fiona, with tear-filled eyes screamed loudly as the three of them braced themselves for the crash, but instead, a great transformation took place in front of their eyes.

Just as the Range Rover hit the Fengall leader, his solid tree trunk-like body began to stretch out like a giant rubber band. His arms flew wide as he grasped hold of the sides of the vehicle as though he was trying to pull it off him. The vehicle shook and Fergo thought he was going to turn the car over, but then they all watched in disbelief as Hawkshead's angry expression was suddenly replaced by a look of horror. His features began to stretch until finally, he was no longer recognisable. The last thing the three saw was terror in his saucer-like eyes as his head snapped back and he disappeared under the car.

"We've run him over!" Fiona screamed as the car finally lurched to a halt. "But where did he go?" They all stared out the back window expecting to see his prone body but instead, all they saw was a snowy white barn owl flutter up from underneath the car. For a moment it circled around uncertainly and then it flew back towards the Gate of Fengall.

In that instant, the rest of the advancing Fengall warriors halted in their tracks. They too had seen the transformation of their great leader. They watched horrified as the white owl flew away, making for the safety of Fengall. Forgetting the three terrified children in the car, the Fengall warriors dropped their weapons and turned and ran screaming back towards the Gate of Fengall after their fleeing leader.

But there were so many of them that they could not all fit through the archway at once. Stones began to rain down on them as the crumbling archway, pounded by a mass of bodies, finally cracked from top to bottom and fell into a pile of rubble. In the chaos, only a few of the warriors had made it through but what they faced now was a barrage of quakes and tremors as the whole foundation of Fengall began to destruct from its very core. The rest of the warriors, stranded on the wrong side, began to writhe around in agony. Then like their leader, they too transformed. Birds of all sizes, shapes and colours flew up into the air, their wings flapping into each other in their attempt to escape. They flew in all directions, circling about not knowing which way to turn, now that Fengall had ceased to exist.

13
Escape

Jamie, Fiona and Fergo clambered out of the battered vehicle.

"We better get out of here. Murphy could be out there still," Fiona said but as she gazed around her, the landscape seemed quiet and deserted. She allowed her tired legs to sink to the ground and Fergo dropped down beside her.

"But which way is home?" asked Fergo.

They stared about them in the darkness knowing they would have to make a choice. They couldn't stay where they were.

"Who knows! There are no landmarks," Fiona remarked.

For several minutes they stood dejectedly, too exhausted to consider what to do next. Then they simply picked a direction that they thought might be the right one and started to walk. They had only been walking for ten minutes, when they heard a noise that put a chill into their hearts. It was the roar of an engine, and the only one it could be was the engine in Murphy's Range Rover.

Without speaking, they tried to run as best they could for it was too dark to make out the rabbit holes and hidden ditches until it was too late. But they could hear that with every step, the engine noise behind them was getting louder. They were too exhausted to go any faster than a walking pace. Fiona wiped tears from her eyes and struggled on; Fergo knew it wouldn't be long before he could not take another step. Jamie, his breath coming now in painful bursts, had to concentrate on keeping his feet going one in front of the other. Then, like a beacon through the darkness, over to the east they saw a light coming towards them.

The three of them stopped in their tracks and turned to look. "Who can that be?" Jamie asked. "No one knows we're out here."

They had changed direction so many times it was impossible to tell which way they were going. There was no way of telling where these lights were coming from. It might have been from Fengall for all they knew, but they knew it could not be Murphy who with every passing minute was getting closer and closer behind them. It was at that moment that the darkness was lit up by the single beam from Murphy's one undamaged headlight. Then they heard the car horn and they knew that Murphy was right behind them.

"Run for it!" Fiona shouted, and holding each other they ran as fast as they could, each making sure the others stayed on their feet. They began to shout and then wave their arms and soon a beam of torchlight flickered on to their faces. With the headlight showing their path they could just make out who approached them. Out of the gloom strode a group of people, several wearing fluorescent stripes on their jackets. Jamie read the word 'Police' and then just behind him, he saw his mum and Fergo's dad. Spread out behind them across the moor came a whole search and rescue team.

"HELP," screamed Jamie for at that moment the Range Rover roared up behind them.

The policeman shouted and began to run towards the three of them, and Murphy seeing the uniform swerved and skidded the vehicle to a halt, missing the three by barely an inch.

Jamie hit the ground and rolled just in time to see Murphy's battered face illuminated in the searchers' torchlights. His eyes were crazed and wild and his face clawed and scratched, as were the faces of his two men who stared out of the windows at them. The Range Rover's paint was scratched and peeling, while still attached under the windscreen wipers were the long black feathers which had once been lethal Fengall spears. It looked like a chariot that had been driven from hell.

None of them breathed as Murphy stared down at Jamie, his unblinking eyes filled with malice. Then the door opened and he got out and reached down towards them. A shout came and Murphy looked up to see that the policeman was now very close. He jumped back into the car, and slamming the door, gunned the engine loudly before shooting off into the dark night like a hunted demon.

Within seconds the three children were surrounded by their families, their faces pale and sick with worry. They hugged each other tightly.

"Thank goodness you are safe. We've been so worried," said Jamie's mother. "It was the postman who told us that Murphy had chased you from the house. Everyone has been out looking all day, but then half way across the moor the mist came in and all signs ran out. It was as though you had just disappeared into thin air."

"How did you know we were out here?" Fiona asked.

"That old Professor from the curio shop was the one who showed us where you might be."

"Is he here with you?" Jamie asked looking out anxiously across the moor.

"Yes, he was right behind us a minute ago. He insisted on coming out to find you."

At that moment out of the mist the old Professor appeared leaning heavily on a wooden stick. He was out of breath but struggling along as best he could. Jamie clutched the pendant in his hand and held the scorched rucksack close to his body as the Professor raised the wooden stick and quickened his pace towards him.

Jamie walked towards the Professor leaving the others behind. When they were a few strides apart, he stopped and glanced anxiously up at the old man but Jamie was relieved to see that the Professor's face was filled with a warm and friendly smile.

"Jamie, are you all all right?" he asked full of concern. "This was my fault. I should have stopped you from going but the owl's power was more devastating than anything I could ever have imagined."

"It's okay. We managed to find Fengall on our own," Jamie whispered making sure his mum and rest of the party were out of earshot.

The Professor gasped. "So you returned the owl?"

Jamie nodded. "Yes, but it was all a trap. You were right. If we had had the last pages of parchment maybe we would have known that all the Fengalls needed was for me to break the spell on the gate so that they could get access to this world. They knew that once the owl's crystal egg had restored their power, they could seek their revenge on us."

"So what happened to the Ebony Owl?" the Professor asked.

"It was destroyed," he said. "Now no one can get their hands on it."

The Professor gave a deep sigh. "It is for the best. Who knows what evil would have come from it."

Jamie didn't get a chance to say any more as his mum and the others came over with hot tea. His mum was in tears as she hugged both her children. "We thought you had been kidnapped," she said as she held them close.

"We were sort of," Fiona began but saw it was the wrong thing to say when her mother let out a wail.

Behind them Fergo was explaining to his father how he had lost his bike.

"That's all right lad, we'll get you a new one. That Murphy will pay for it as well," his father said angrily.

Then after a reviving drink and a few minutes rest, the police vehicles arrived to take them back to the warmth and comfort of their homes in Craiginver.

14
The Last Flight

That night, for the first time in a long time, Jamie had a pleasant dream. It felt like the first peaceful sleep he could remember in his whole eleven years. He woke up to hear Fiona messing about next door in her room and he slowly went over all that had happened. His mind began to relive their time in Fengall until finally he came to the part of their escape. Only then did he remember the crystal egg.

He jumped from his bed and ran to his rucksack. He opened the pocket slowly and looked inside. There, lying in the bottom among the dust and dirt, was the solid milk-white stone.

"It's so cold," he muttered to himself as he picked it up.

He got dressed and went downstairs taking the crystal over to the sink in the kitchen to rinse it. He heard Fiona come down behind him and he turned to her looking very guilty.

"What's the matter?" she asked him.

He didn't know how to tell her. "I've still got Fengall's crystal egg."

"You have *what*? Jamie what have you done!" she screeched.

"But it's all right. With Fengall gone, it's just a rock," insisted Jamie, and with that he showed it to her only to see something which nearly frightened the life out of him. Under the water, the crystal had changed colour.

"What's happening?" he yelled.

"Don't tell me it's hatching," said Fiona peering over Jamie's shoulder. But instead of being a smooth milk-white stone, it was now a bright, clear crystal. They both gaped at it in astonishment.

"Remember what Murphy said? He thought it could be worth a fortune!" Jamie exclaimed.

At that moment Fergo appeared at the back door. He gasped and gave a loud hoot when he saw the bright crystal Jamie was holding on his outstretched palm. It looked like the biggest diamond he had ever seen. He couldn't take his eyes off it. "If that's a diamond we could all be very rich!" Then he began to hop about singing at the top of his voice, just as Jamie's mum came into the kitchen.

"What on earth is going on here?" she asked just as Fergo spun out of control hitting the kitchen counter and knocking over the fruit bowl. Then she noticed Jamie standing with his hands behind his back, looking very secretive.

"What have you got there?" she asked.

"Nothing, Mum," Jamie replied.

"Jamie? Show me what you are hiding behind your back."

Jamie gave in. "We found this crystal...we think it could be valuable, maybe even a diamond! If it was, it could be the answer to all our problems," Jamie said opening out the palm of his hand to reveal the stone to his mother but when his fingers opened, the crystal had returned to its dull milky colour. It looked just like a stone egg again.

"Very funny, Jamie. A rock collection is about all you could start with that," she said dismissing the stone with one glance. "Now keep the noise down will you. I've just heard that the police have spotted Murphy outside London. I don't think he'll be coming back here for a while."

The three looked at each other knowingly but before their mum could get a chance to ask why, the phone went. Mrs Logan went off to answer it and Fergo took the stone from Jamie's hand. Instantly, it transformed back into a bright, sparkling crystal.

"What shall we do with it?" asked Jamie quietly. He glanced at Fiona.

"Get rid of it, Jamie," she said. "Before we get into any more trouble."

"But if it is a rare crystal, even more rare than a

diamond, it could be worth millions," Fergo commented. "Fengall doesn't need it any more."

"Then we could sell it and buy Mum a big, new café of her own," said Jamie, "and move to a bigger house."

But Fiona shook her head. "Don't get your hopes up...What about the Professor? He might know what to do."

"Okay, let's go see him," Fergo replied.

News travels fast in small villages so they didn't get far before they were being asked how they were.

"We hear Murphy's on the run because of you," one man said patting Jamie on the back, but it was one of Fergo's friends who told them that Murphy had been caught. It seemed that the three of them had accomplished more than just destroying the Fengall threat. When the police had searched Murphy's house for clues as to the children's whereabouts, they had found stolen jewels and antiques hidden in the attic. The whole house had been cordoned off and a police hunt had started for the errant Murphy. All work on the marina had stopped after one of Murphy's men had told the police about the secret cave. An archaeologist was examining the site and had decided that there was a significant burial chamber hidden deep within the cliff. Not only was it filled with old Scottish relics but some fragments had been found from a strange unknown civilisation.

Feeling quite jubilant at this news of Murphy's capture, they completely forgot about seeing the Professor as they hurried to the seafront to see the cave for themselves. But on their way, the feeling of good humour died when they came across the group of angry people standing on the pier.

Everyone was standing around a man whose face was pale and stricken, but this time it wasn't Angus, but a young American tourist.

"That old guy was right," he was shouting. "There really is something up there. I've seen it with my own eyes!" he said pointing to the cliffs. "Boy, it was weird. It was a tall masked man dressed in the most bizarre clothes. I think we should tell the police, let them deal with it."

Then they noticed old Angus standing on the outside of the circle shaking his head knowingly. "Maybe now you'll take me seriously," he said.

Jamie felt a coldness creep through him as he gazed at the crowd who seemed intent on doing something about it themselves.

"Let's go up there and have a look ourselves. Find out what's really going on," a voice in the crowd shouted. "We can't have folk scared to walk our cliffs." There were other shouts of agreement.

Jamie edged away from the crowd dragging Fergo and Fiona back with him, but at that moment he spotted Professor Moncrieff who had been leaning against a wall listening to what everyone had to say.

"Jamie, what is this I hear?" he said ambling over. "You told me that Fengall had been destroyed. That warrior should no longer be here."

"Fengall was destroyed. We saw it happen...didn't we?" Jamie turned to the others for support.

"Jamie, you'd better tell the Professor..." Fiona began.

"Tell me what?" the Professor asked.

"I took it. I completely forgot I had it in all the rush," Jamie told him, and from his bag he brought out the crystal egg.

"Och, *no*, Jamie. If that had been left inside Fengall when the gate fell it would have been destroyed too. What have you done?"

"Does that warrior know we have the crystal egg then?" Fiona whispered to Fergo. "How can it? We saw Fengall destroyed with our own eyes!"

Fergo declared. "That warrior shouldn't even be alive!"

"As long as you have the crystal then a wee bit of Fengall must still exist. It must emit just enough power for the warrior to remain here," the Professor said.

Jamie's face had lost all its colour. "So things aren't over yet," he said. He looked into his sister's frightened face.

"Maybe we should just let the warrior have the egg and be done with it?" Fiona suggested.

Fergo's eyes grew wide. "*What?* Just hand it over. After all we've been through!"

But then an idea flickered around inside Jamie's mind. He looked up at the Professor, who seemed to know what he was thinking. Jamie turned back to the others.

"I have to go back up to the cliffs one last time," he told them. Then he glanced at the crowd. Now there was talk of going up armed with spades, garden forks, and anything else they could lay their hands on. There wasn't much time before they took the matter into their own hands. Who knows what would happen if he didn't get there first?

"Go on Jamie, I'll handle things here," the Professor said to him. Jamie broke away from the others, the crystal egg gripped firmly in his hand.

"Hey, Jamie come back. Where are you going?" Fiona shouted running after him. "We're in this together."

Jamie waited for the two to catch him up and then they jogged off along the pier leaving the Professor trying to pacify the crowd. There was a short cut up to the cliffs which required clambering up through brambles and nettles but would give them precious minutes in case the Professor was unable to stop the crowd coming after them.

The first signs of autumn were already in the air as they walked the path that had led them into such danger only days before.

"Your mum would kill us if she knew we were coming back up here," said Fergo as he pulled his coat tightly around his body. Soon they could hear the waves crashing on the rocks beneath them. The leaves in the birch trees around them were beginning to turn yellow and crisp. The tinge of autumn was apparent in every branch. A cool breeze blew a mass of leaves across the path as the sun filtered down weakly through the branches. Summer was finally over for another year.

"What are you going to do, Jamie?" Fiona asked, shivering violently as they reached the place where they had encountered the warrior before.

"The egg has to be destroyed," Jamie replied determinedly, but then he looked down at the crystal and sighed. "Doesn't look like Mum will be getting her new café after all."

They had taken only a few more steps when the lone warrior came into view, walking along the path towards them with the black raven flying above, cawing loudly out over the cliffs. The light from the warrior's mask was now very pale and it was no longer strong enough to radiate out over the sea. They watched as it stopped on the cliff edge to allow the raven to settle back on to its shoulder. They could see that the warrior had nearly faded away though the raven remained very much alive. It sensed that something was wrong and refused to stop its incessant cawing.

All three of them stopped in their tracks. "There it is," said Jamie.

"What are you going to do now?" Fergo asked.

But Jamie didn't answer. Instead, he began to walk towards the warrior. Fergo and Fiona followed slowly behind, not sure of what Jamie had in mind as he strode boldly towards the cliff edge. The raven turned its beady eye at his approach and started to flap its wings before it flew up into the air, calling out a warning to the warrior.

The Fengall warrior turned its head slowly towards them and the now faint beam of light that had probed the horizon turned to shine on Jamie's face. Jamie was so close that he could see the strange face behind the mask and even though he was shaking from head to toe with fear, he kept moving forward. Slowly, from his jacket pocket, he drew out the crystal.

"This is all that's left of Fengall," Jamie shouted at the warrior. Then holding out the sparkling stone in one hand and clutching his pendant tightly in the other, he broke into a run heading straight for the cliff edge.

Fergo screamed out, "Jamie, what are you doing?" Fiona made a grab at the back of Jamie's jacket but her fingers slipped off the material as he sprinted forward. The warrior had seen the stone and as Jamie ran towards him, it brought its lance down ready to strike. But Jamie took no notice until he was within yards of being stabbed by the sharp tip. Then he stopped in his tracks and, using all his strength, he threw the crystal as hard as he could.

The tall warrior watched spellbound, as the sparkling crystal flew up in a huge arc over its head and then spun out over the edge of the cliff. It raised its hand and tried to snatch the crystal as it passed overhead, but its long claw-like fingers clicked on nothing but thin air.

Then, with an enraged cry, as the warrior launched itself from the cliff after the crystal that was still curving outwards in an enormous curve towards the sea.

Things seemed to go into slow motion as Jamie, Fiona and Fergo rushed forwards just in time to see the raven, dislodged from the warrior's shoulder, flap uncertainly up into the air and then fly out to sea.

When they reached the cliff edge they saw the warrior plummeting down towards the jagged rocks below. Fiona screamed in horror as she imagined what was about to happen, but then the transformation took place. The warrior's feathered cloak suddenly changed into a mighty set of black wings and then its whole body altered in shape. Spared by inches from death on the rocks, a huge bald eagle soared up into the air. After several strokes of its mighty wings it flew straight out to sea after the fast disappearing black raven.

They all heard the warrior's spear clatter down on to the rocks and disappear in the white crashing sea. With the crystal egg gone, their eyes were fixed on the two birds who were fast becoming specks in the distance. The big black body of the eagle with its slow majestic strokes glided straight towards the sun, while the black raven, flying beneath it had to beat its wings rapidly to keep up with its companion.

"That's the last we'll see of the Fengalls," Jamie said turning to the others.

They walked away from the cliff edge and headed back down the path. It was then that they met the little party of villagers on their way up to search the cliffs.

"Have you seen any ghostly beasties up here?" one of the men armed with a spade asked.

"No, we haven't seen anything," Jamie replied glancing at the other two. "There's nothing happening up here at all."

The party halted by the cliff edge and Jamie, Fergo and Fiona went on their way. No one noticed the snowy white owl perched silently in the trees above them. The early autumn breeze blew through the branches, ruffling its feathers and making it grip tightly to the swaying branch. It looked down at the group of people with its hooded green eyes and blinked as it watched Jamie throw his pendant up into the air where for a moment it spun in the sunlight before dropping back into his outstretched palm. The owl blinked again, glaring at them from under its feathery brows. Jamie and Fiona ran off down the cliff path laughing, while Fergo pelted along behind them, his long coat tails flapping out behind him.